# DARK POISON

# DEDICATION

To all my OG readers,
The ones with me from the start,
This one is for you.
Thank you xx

# DARK POISON

All rights reserved. This eBook is licensed for your personal enjoyment only. This eBook is copyright material and must not be copied, reproduced, transferred, distributed, leased, licensed or publicly performed or used in any form without prior written permission of the publisher, as allowed under the terms and conditions under which it was purchased or as strictly permitted by applicable copyright law. Any unauthorized distribution, circulation or use of this text may be a direct infringement of the author's rights, and those responsible may be liable in law accordingly. Thank you for respecting the work of this author.

DARK POISON
Copyright © 2022 Bella Jewel

DARK POISON is a work of fiction. All names, characters, places and events portrayed in this book either are from the author's imagination or are used fictitiously. Any similarity to real persons, living or dead, establishments, events, or location is purely coincidental and not intended by the author.

## ACKNOWLEDGMENTS

As always, my heartfelt thanks to every single blogger, reader and author that has supported my journey. From reading my books, to sharing them, to raving about them, to being there for me. Thank you. My career would be nothing without any of you.

A massive thanks to the team at Valentine PR for taking me on, especially to Kim and Nina for helping me with this release and this new series. I am looking forward to working with you all on this book and future books, and I'm incredibly grateful for the hard work you all do.

A massive thanks to Ben Ellis from Tall Story Designs for this gorgeous cover. You're the easiest, most efficient person I've ever worked with. You make my covers absolutely gorgeous every single time. I couldn't do it without you.

To my favorite editor Wendi from Ready, set, edit, for always coming through for me on my edits, whenever I need them. You're amazing and I'm so thankful to you. You're super easy to work with and so nice. I'm glad to team up with you for these things.

And of course, to my admin, MJ, for ALWAYS keeping my page running beautifully. I couldn't do it without you, girly. I love your teasers and your passion; thank you for taking the time out of your life to help this poor girl keep everything running.

To all of my readers that started with me as Bec Botefuhr – I know you'll cherish this rewrite as much as I do. I hope you enjoy it every bit as much as the first and thank you for being with me this whole time.

And, last but certainly not least, to my loyal readers. To each and every one of you that picks up my books and give me a chance. To the reviews you write, good or bad. To the time you take to make me a better person. You make this real for me; never stop giving such love and passion. You make our journey so amazing.

# PROLOGUE

I run my fingers through the damp soil as I sit on the grass, the dew soaking into my long, black dress as I stare at the empty gravesite. Nobody is here, nobody except me and my mother. The silence is deafening as the priest murmurs a few incoherent words. Rain drops splatter on my father's faded-brown casket, the only one we could afford. It would have been nicer — could have been nicer — if my mother hadn't used all our savings to fuel her drug habit.

Death has a feeling. An empty, soul-crushing feeling. Even when you say your final goodbyes, your very being is dragged down into the dirt with your loved one. My father, he was the only good thing I had left. Now it's just her and me. She doesn't love me. Perhaps once she did, but, for right now, her only care in this bitter world is when she can get her next hit. He fought for us. He fought for me.

"Get up off the ground, Willow," comes her scolding voice as she reaches down, her bony fingers curling around my arm as she hauls me on to my feet.

She still speaks to me as if I'm a small child. Like the world hasn't crushed me because of her sins. I might not be old enough to escape her clutches, but my mind far outweighs others of my age.

She still acts as though I don't understand.

"Don't touch me," I murmur, staring as the casket slowly lowers into the ground.

The creaking sounds from the machine doing all the work only make the entire situation more eerie. I cross my arms and stare down, watching as the only good thing in my life gets lowered into the ground. I'll never be able to talk to him again, never be able to hear his voice or feel his presence. He's gone, and he left me when I needed him the most. For that, I hate him.

"Do not scold me at your father's funeral," she hisses, leaning in close. "I've lost everything because of you."

Because of me.

Because. Of. Me.

She thinks this is my fault.

The problem with that is … she's wrong.

He was just going to get me some ice cream. He hugged me, kissed me, told me he loved me, and then disappeared.

He never came home.

There was an accident — his car went right off the side of the road, down a large ditch, and then was thrown over a cliff.

It's my fault, according to her, because I wanted the ice cream.

If she wasn't passed out in her room, she could have gotten it for me.

"The only thing you've lost, Mother," I whisper, shivering as the cold feels like it goes down to my very bones, "is the ability to live."

She stares at me and then shakes her head. "I can't do this anymore, not with you. You need to go somewhere else. Without him ..."

Without him, she has no money.

That means she has no drugs.

That means she has to find a way to get money, and she's not going to spend a single cent of that on me.

I'm not scared; no, I no longer care if I'm with her or I'm not.

He took a piece of me when he left me.

There is nothing more for her to break.

# 1

Flashing lights flicker as bodies move across the dance floor. Laughter and the sounds of glasses clinking can be heard as we shimmy through the sea of bodies. It's a vibe, and only the kind of vibe you get from the most elite of clubs. This one, newly opened, is the best of the best, and people have flocked for miles to get in. Luckily for us, my best friend Ava knows people and managed to secure us a way in tonight.

I'm grateful.

It's incredible.

"This place is bustling," I yell to Ava as we shove through the crowds of people trying to find a space to settle in.

"I know. It's pretty cool, right? Mark told me this is the place to be."

I nod my head. "It's impressive, your boss knows his stuff."

I glance around as we move closer and closer to the bar; it's something else entirely, with the flashing neon lights, blue and purple, and the crystal-clear glass chandeliers hanging from the ceiling.

We manage to make it to the bar and find ourselves a gap big enough to try our hand at getting a drink. Ava turns to me, a smile on her face. "Club life, eh?"

I laugh, nodding. "Yeah. It's something else."

Ava grins and tosses her long, blond hair over her shoulder, looking around. "There are some fine men in here tonight."

I glance around. The girl is right, there most certainly are. I could use a night out with one of these hotties.

"I say we make a bet," Ava yells over the blaring music.

I raise my brows. "Oh?"

A wicked grin spreads across her face. "I say it'll be ten minutes before we're served. If I'm right, you pay."

I chuckle. "Alright, I'll play your little game. I say it'll be five minutes because we're so dammed fine."

Ava throws her head back and laughs, and then she reaches over and shakes my hand. "Deal."

I've known Ava since we were just ten years old, and we've been inseparable since. Completely opposite in looks and personality, we couldn't be more different, and, yet, it works for us. She's the only person I've ever had when things went bad in my life, and I couldn't do it without her.

Ava is beautiful in the kind of way that stops men in their tracks. It's not just her gorgeous figure, the blond hair, and the blue eyes, but the fact that when she laughs, it's infectious. She has this vibe that draws you to her and makes you never want to leave. She's bubbly and the light of every room she's in.

So, when I hear the deep, husky voice behind me offering a drink, I'm assuming the man speaking is talking to Ava. Why wouldn't he be? She's in a tight black dress and has legs to God knows where. I'm the opposite, wearing short denim pants and a tank top that's a little too tight. My hair is a dark shade of red, and my eyes are emerald green. My hair has always been what makes me stand out from a crowd, but when I'm beside Ava, all that disappears because she's … well … Ava.

"Did you hear me, lady? Can I buy you a drink?"

He's not speaking to Ava, he's speaking to *me*.

I turn slowly and come face to face with one of the most spectacular men I have ever had the pleasure of laying my eyes on.

He's everything I'd usually go for. The tall, dark, and handsome is strong in this one. His hair is messy, little strands of it falling around his face, and in here, it looks to be almost black.

His eyes are light blue, so light they look like glass, like you could just see right through them. His skin is that creamy olive, like warm milk and coffee, and his body ... Oh, his body. The guy is massive, and I don't say that lightly. He's a good six foot something of pure, solid muscle.

Man is fine.

"Me?"

I sound stupid, I know I do. But men like him, they don't usually come to me first. Ava has turned around beside me and her brows are raised as she stares as the man standing before me. When she pulls her bottom lip into her mouth, I know what she's thinking, this man is fucking fire.

"Yeah you, beautiful."

Beautiful?

Is he serious?

I've been called a few things in my time, I can't say beautiful is one of the words that comes up often.

Ava nudges me when I stand there, not saying a damned word, just staring like a love-struck teenager.

I get it together.

"I'll have vodka and tonic."

The man smirks at me, the little side lift of his lips that makes me weak at the knees. I can't say I've seen a man that looks like him in quite some time. Not taking my eyes off him, I watch as he turns and slams his hand down onto the bar. The bartender immediately rushes over as if there aren't a shit load of other people waiting.

"What can I get you, sir?"

Sir? Last time I checked, no one called anyone sir in a club, like ever. Mystery man leans over the bar and puts in an order, and the bartender rushes off right away after giving him a sharp nod. I stare at the tattoos running up his arms as he leans on the bar, some Celtic design, a mix of patterns and dark shades. It's very appealing. So is the tight dark shirt and black jeans he's sporting. Don't get me started on the boots. He's a bad boy, and he is making sure everyone knows it.

Ava leans in and whispers in my ear. "Oh my, girl, if you don't ride that all the way home, I will."

I grin and nudge her. "I'm still in shock. Do you think he's blind?"

Ava glowers at me, crossing her arms. "You're fucking gorgeous and the man is not blind, he's into you. You better take him home, or trust me, someone else will."

She's right. This one won't last long.

Still, he's picking me? Why?

"Seriously, though," she whispers into my ear, her hand on my arm so she can get in close, "how long has it been since you've had sex?"

Ugh. Don't even. The last time was with Danny, my long-term boyfriend. Not only was he shit in bed, but the man was an abusive prick. He had a temper that far outmatched my own and he made sure I knew that I belonged to him and nobody else. To the point that when he found me out one night, dancing with my friends, he hit me.

That was the end of that for me.

I ended it and hauled ass out of there. I haven't heard from him since.

But, to her point, the sex scene has been pretty damned mild for me.

I purse my lips. "Danny."

She curls her mouth in disgust. "Ugh, that pompous ass. Yuck."

"Here's your drink."

I turn again to face the crystal-blue eyes that have no doubt lured many women to some serious orgasms. This man ... this man knows how to fuck. It's written all over him. From head to toe, he makes it known he could take your body and do wicked things with it. I reach out with trembling fingers and take the drink, flashing my very best smile.

Ava gives me a thumbs up over his shoulder, before disappearing into the crowd to dance.

"You dance?" he murmurs, sipping his drink.

"That depends," I answer, taking a big gulp of mine.

Very lady like.

"On what?"

I grin. "How good you are at dancing, because if you're good enough, it'll hide how bad I am and nobody will notice."

His grin gets bigger.

Oh god.

"Let's see how we go, then."

He takes my hand and leads me onto the dance floor. I feel giddy and nervous all at the same time. Mystery man takes my hips in his hands the second we find a clear spot, and he starts swaying my body in an effortless movement. Not only does he smell fucking good, but his body is hard and strong. He pulls me closer, until we're pressed together, and it takes everything inside of me not to moan, because god damn, I'm enjoying every second of this.

Leaning down, his lips brush across my ear, making me shiver. "What's your name?"

"Willow," I murmur, closing my eyes and enjoying every god damned second of this.

"Fuckin' beautiful."

Oh.

Yes.

Song after song passes, and he seems to be fixed on me and only me. His hands roam my body, his mouth grazes my neck, and yet at no point does he kiss me or attempt to take things to the next level. It's like he's keeping me on the end of a rope, pulling just enough to stop me from leaving. I want more, and he's not giving me more.

I'm not about to give up on the night, though. Oh no.

I want this man, and I'm going to make sure he tugs that damned rope hard enough that we come crashing together.

"I need to use the bathroom," I murmur, when yet another song finishes.

He nods. "I'll get more drinks."

He releases me and turns, striding through the crowd, his presence strong and powerful. People step aside, moving without thought. I watch him go, eyes narrowed as I notice he doesn't once look at any other woman who tries desperately to get his attention, and there are quite a few of them. They're all beautiful. It seems odd. Out of all the girls he chose to zone in on tonight, why did he pick me?

"How's it going?"

Ava sidles up to me, her face glistening with sweat, her eyes glassy from alcohol. I take her arm and tug her out of the crowd and toward the bathroom, desperate to pee. I do my business and, once I'm done, I pull her into the corner.

"He seems overly fixated on me."

"And? What's the problem? You're gorgeous and he knows it. You should be flattered."

"Seriously, though, have you seen the other women out there? They're fucking beautiful and throwing themselves at him. He's not even looking in their direction. It just seems ... odd."

Ava frowns. "You don't think he's some sort of stalker or something?"

I laugh, rolling my eyes. "Jesus, no. At least, I don't think so."

She gives me a look, crossing her arms. "Well, if I don't see you later, I'll know where you are."

I nod. "At least my kidnapper is hot."

She laughs. "Come on, you've got some work to do. You're taking that man home."

Oh, indeed.

I return to the dance floor, and he shows up with two drinks in hand, his eyes slowly moving over my body, taking me in. He just spent the last hour with his hands on every inch of me, and yet he's studying me like it's the first time he's truly paid attention. When his eyes finally meet mine, he grins. Small, but oh, so fucking sexy.

"Should we sit down?" I ask.

He steps in closer. "I'm not done with you."

Oh boy.

He hands me my drink, and I throw it down without even tasting it. Then I'm in his arms again, his body doing things to me that I'm not sure I can ignore a whole lot longer. Everything inside me aches, and I know for certain I need this man to take me home tonight. It has been too long, and he's exactly what I need.

"What do you do for a living?" he murmurs into my ear as his hand runs down my back, slowly, making my skin prickle.

"I was an office assistant, but at the moment I don't have a job."

"Nice."

"What about you?"

His blue eyes sparkle with amusement — what did I say that was so funny?

"Just a mechanic."

That's it?

He seems like so much more than that.

"What's your name?"

I haven't asked him that question yet, and it's in that moment I realize I'm getting a little too drunk, and if we don't leave soon, I'll probably end up sick and ruin all my chances of a wicked night with this man. My head is feeling light, and I'm spinning a lot more than I was ten minutes ago. That last drink must have been strong, and I drank it way too fast.

"Johnny."

Fuck me.

Of course he has a hot name.

"Want to get some fresh air?"

He nods.

As we move through the crowd, with them stepping aside for him, I notice I'm struggling to keep my footing. Why do I feel so lightheaded? I was fine ten minutes ago, getting tipsy, sure, but not drunk to the point I'm struggling to walk. I might be a lightweight but, man, this is bad even for me. Johnny escorts me down the hall with his hand on the small of my back, occasionally stopping me from falling. He's so scarily calm, moving me through the crowd as if I'm not stumbling and tripping over myself.

"Come on, you need some water."

He's right about that.

I pause and close my eyes, trying to figure out what the hell has gone wrong. When I open them again, I see two of him. Well, this can't be good.

"Something is wrong, how strong was that drink?" I slur.

Is that my voice?

God.

"You've just had too much. When you're dancing in the dark, it doesn't feel like you're as drunk as you really are. Fresh air will help."

Something is wrong.

Alarm bells are going off in my head. I didn't drink so much that I would be this drunk. Where's Ava? Did she see us leave? Why do we have to walk all the way out here for fresh air when we could have just gone out the front? I try to pull my hand from his with no success. I'm too drunk and he's too strong. I'm unable to get one foot in front of the other, let alone escape his hold. I trip and tumble forward, but he catches me with zero effort, hauling me up into his arms.

That's when I know the situation I'm in is dangerous.

"Let me go," I slur, struggling to even focus on where we are as he begins striding off toward the darkness.

He doesn't answer.

My attempts at getting him to put me down are futile.

My words go unnoticed.

With every passing step, my vision blurs even more, and I can't fight it any longer.

Everything goes black.

~*~*~*~

They say instinct tells you when something is wrong, or your gut, whichever you'd like to go with.

I know something is wrong the moment I open my eyes.

Outside of the fact that my head is pounding, my vision is blurry, and I feel like I'm going to vomit. It takes me a moment to gather my bearings, and when I do, I know I'm not at home. No, not even close.

I'm in a room that, upon first glance, would appear completely normal. A bed, a bathroom and toilet, a desk in the corner, clean, tidy, very normal looking. That is, of course, until you cast your eyes over to the window that is barred with large metal poles, or the door that was obviously once wooden, and is now a solid steel with a keypad to enter and exit. This isn't just any room, this is a prison cell.

I gasp in shock and pull my arms, only to realize not only am I in a stranger's fucking prison room but I'm tied up. I twist my head to the side, trying to see where the rope I'm connected to goes, but I can't see a damned thing. I jerk my hands again, and the rope allows just enough room for me to squirm into a sitting position, but that's as far as I can go.

Fear lurches in my chest as I stare around again and the events of the night before come crawling back into my mind. Johnny, the mystery man who was overly focused on me. He spent the entire evening making sure I was the only one he gave his attention to, and then, he was carrying me away into the darkness as I fought to regain control. He drugged me. He fucking drugged me.

Is he a god damned rapist? Murderer? What the hell is he going to do with me?

A sick feeling swarms my stomach, and I jerk again, desperately trying to escape the rope, but there is no use, they're secured too well.

The sounds of the keys on the keypad beeping has me whipping my head toward the door. A moment later a small click rings out and it opens. I'm faced with the perfect face of the man I spent the night dancing with, grinding my body against, and imagining a wild night beneath the sheets. This is certainly not the kind of bed scenario I was conjuring up.

In the light of day, he looks even more spectacular, and I curse myself for only thinking of my vagina last night. If I had used my brain, I would have realized there was something off with this godly looking man. Sporting only a pair of jeans, I can see that his size is far more incredible than I could have imagined last night. He's covered in tattoos and his body ... god his body. Perhaps we did sleep together and this is some sort of BDSM bullshit?

His eyes scan over me and then he turns to lock the door behind him, and I see across his back, in big, black letters he has tattooed 'JAGGER.'

Is that his nickname? Or maybe he's a die-hard fan of Mick Jagger.

Stranger things have happened. He walks over to the bed, his gaze raking over me. He doesn't look like a rapist or a murderer, but that's not to say he isn't. Sometimes the best looking men are the most dangerous.

"What," I rasp out, "the actual fuck is going on here?"

I need water. Stat.

He raises a brow and his lip twitches. Okay, so maybe we did have sex and played dirty little games, and I just can't remember? God, what a damned pity. That is a memory I would love to get back.

"You're here because I need you to be."

Doesn't answer my question.

"Did we …"

I raise my brows.

His eyes widen, and his face turns stone hard. All humor is gone from his dark depths.

"I didn't fuck you," he grinds out. "I have no intentions of fucking you. Is that what you think this is? You think I tied you up and put you in a secured room because I'm some sort of twisted motherfucker?"

"It makes sense," I throw back. "Why else would I be tied up?"

He glares at me. "You're here, Willow, because your father has some very vital information, and we need to get him out of hiding."

I blink.

The man is delusional. I think he's somehow gotten me confused for someone else. My father is dead.

"Hate to break it to you, pal, but my father is dead. Can you please release me? It's clear you've got the wrong woman."

"No, he's not. He's in Witness Protection because he delved in some shady fuckin' business and ran with information my boys and I need."

His boys? What the hell is this?

"Is this some sort of joke?"

His face remains stony. "Do I look like I'm joking?"

He doesn't look like he's joking, and any humor left in my body slowly shrinks away as I realize the situation I'm in could end very very badly if I'm not careful. Whoever this man is, he's obviously bad, and I'm not about to stick around to find out just how bad he is. I need to get out of here. He has the wrong person. The quicker I can prove that, the quicker he lets me go.

"My father is dead," I say again. "He died. I watched him get lowered into the ground. You have the wrong person."

"That's what they want you to think. He was in danger and they needed everyone to believe he was no longer alive. I assure you, Willow, he is. He's in protection, and I need him to come out."

"You're wrong."

"But I'm not. You're here because I need you to get him out."

This can't be happening. There must be some mistake. Could my father really be alive? Could he have been in protection this whole time? If so, why wouldn't he have found a way to let me know? Was he really in so much danger that he couldn't, at the very least, stop my suffering by telling me he's alive?

My chest clenches. "If what you say is true, then what the hell do you need me for?"

He smirks, and I no longer see beauty. Right now, the man standing in front of me is a stone-cold monster. My survival instincts begin taking over. If he's going to hurt me, then he's going to see that I'll fight. I'll fight so god damned hard to make sure he never gets what he wants. Whatever that might be.

"Because when he hears the news of your kidnapping, he will step forward."

That's it? That's his big plan?

I snort. "You're assuming my father loves me."

He grins, low and wicked. "He'll come."

So sure of himself.

"And what if no one reports me missing?" I challenge.

He narrows his eyes. "I know what you're doing, and it won't work. Your family will report this, your best friend will be frantic by now."

He's right. She will. But I'm not about to tell him that.

"My sister doesn't see me often," I say, my voice rough. "It will take her a few weeks to realize something's off. My mother is a drug addict and currently in an institution for the mentally unwell. Ava might report me, but who is going to believe I didn't just run off with some hot guy I met? So tell me, wise guy, how do you suppose this little plan will work?"

Without warning, he lunges forward and grips my face in his hands, leaning in close. His fingers tighten around my jaw, and it takes everything for me not to gasp in pain as the pressure builds. "I would advise you keep your fucking mouth shut. I'm not here to argue with you. I have a plan, and my plan will work. Push me again and you won't like how it ends for you. You're nothing more than a bargaining chip."

He lets go of my face with a shove, and I fall backward. I land on my back with a thump and struggle in my binds but I can't get free;

I've tried, there is no use. He pulls a knife from the back of his jeans and walks over.

With one swift movement he flips me onto my stomach and crushes my head into the pillow with one hand. I curse and squirm, but he's too strong. Heart racing, I brace for whatever it is he's about to do. He tugs, and then I feel him cut the binds before releasing me. I don't dare move. It's a trick, it has to be.

"You can't get out of this room, so don't try," his voice trails in, rough and angry. "We can make this easy or difficult. Do as you're told, and it will hurt a whole lot less. Don't do as you're told, and things will get very fuckin' messy. I don't want to have to go for your sister, but believe me, I'll do whatever I have to do to get what I want."

I don't roll, I just push up on my elbows and stare down at the comforter on the bed.

"My father would do nothing for my sister, she isn't his child," I grind out.

Jenny is a child only a touch younger than me that my mother had when she cheated on my dad. I'll never forget the fights, the anguish, the pain when he found out. But he stuck around, he made it work, he held on because he loved me, he loved her even though she wasn't his. My mother, even during her worst times, had this hold on him. Like he could never let her go.

"No, but you would."

I clamp my eyes shut. Don't cry, be strong. He wants weakness. I refuse to give it to him. If he thinks my father is alive, then time will surely tell. If not, then he'll let me go and I can get the hell out of here. But, one thing is for certain, I will not show a single moment of fear to this man.

I vow it.

"Just leave her out of this," I whisper, angrily.

"Then do as I say and this will run smoothly."

"I don't deserve this," I snap, finding my strength as I roll over and finally face him. "Are you so pathetic that you have to steal an innocent girl just to get some information? Big man."

He leans forward and takes hold of my shoulder with one big hand, jerking me forward. I take the opportunity to kick my leg out, connecting with his hip as hard as I possibly can. Bellowing, he leaps backward, and I roll off the bed and start crawling toward the door. He snarls a curse and spins around, gripping my ankle and pulling me back. I land hard on my stomach but that doesn't mean I'm ready to give up my fight. I kick him again, hitting something I can't see, maybe a shin. He leaps on top of me, his hard weight pinning me to the floor.

"Get off me," I bellow, thrashing my body. "Get the fuck off me."

"You can make this easy or hard on yourself," he says, his breath against my ear, his voice like steel. "I will hurt you. Do not doubt me."

"I'll never give in to you," I seethe. "Mark my words, I will get out of here. You're pathetic."

"Enough," he roars, getting up and hauling me off the ground as he does. He spins me around, and in one, swift movement he has the knife pressed to my throat.

It takes a long moment for me to really grasp the situation, but as the cold steel presses against my neck and I look into the stone cold eyes of the man in front of me, I know he's not lying. He'll do anything to get what he wants, and if that means he has to hurt me, he will. I stare in horror, eyes wide, as the realization sinks in.

He stares at me for a long, long moment before lowering the knife and turning, leaving the room and locking the door behind him. Frustration bubbles in my chest, and I scream, slamming my fists against the door and hurling curses at him, but it's too late, he's gone. I smash my fists into anything I can find, and soon I'm on the ground heaving and crying.

My heaving quickly turns into hyperventilating, and I begin gasping for air. I can't stay here,

I can't be trapped in this room for months … or years.

I claw at the carpet, my body trembling. No matter what I do, I can't force myself to calm down. All this over my father? Who is apparently alive? How could he do this to me? How could he lie? I thought he was dead. I suffered, I grieved.

He was everything to me.

If he's alive …

No.

This has to be a mistake.

When I finally manage to start breathing properly, I crawl to the window and peer out. Heavy bars cover most of the view, but I can see that we are in the middle of nowhere. All I can see for miles and miles are trees. An endless amount of trees. That doesn't mean I'm going to give up, though.

No. I will run through those trees if I can, until I curl up and die from dehydration.

I'd rather that than stay here.

I will get out of here.

I will.

They have picked the wrong girl.

# 2

A long, quiet night passes and nobody comes in. I don't hear a sound; I don't hear a damned thing except the whistling of the trees outside. Wherever we are, there are no towns close by. As I stare out of the barred window, I see nothing but pure darkness. I don't know if he has left or if he's just avoiding me. I don't know what he has in store for me, or even if he's telling the truth. I've replayed it over and over in my mind. Is my father truly alive? And if so, what did he do to get himself into protection?

Mostly, why the hell did he leave me with her? My drug addict mother.

That hurts the most.

When the morning light shines through the window, I drag myself out of the bed and push to my feet, standing in the warmth that is trickling through.

Last night was long, draining. I read the one small book in the room, twice, and sang to myself during the longest, darkest hours of the evening, when my mind was getting the better of me.

I'm not going down the road my mother went. I won't let myself lose control, not of my mind, not of my body. I've been there before, and I didn't like it. Not a single fucking bit.

*"Willow, why do you do this to yourself?" my sister, Jenny, whispers, stroking my hair, her eyes darting around the room, as if the answers lie there.*

*"She makes me crazy," I whimper, trying to pull my hands from the restraints holding me to the bed.*

*Why do they have to tie me? I'm not crazy. I'm not like her.*

*"She's sick. She has a disease. It isn't something you can fix.*

*"She's a monster."*

*"No, honey, she's not. Please, don't do this, don't crumble. I need you."*

*"I can't," I whisper.*

*Neither of us looks down at the damage to my stomach, damage I created myself when my mother made me so crazy I just lost it. I've never felt so desperate in my life. I wanted to hurt her, god, I wanted to hurt her so badly that I ended up hurting myself.*

The beeping sounds of the keypad has my head snapping up and zoning in on the door. He's finally coming in, is he? I don't move from my spot on the floor; instead, I just stand, anxiously waiting.

As the door pushes open, I stare at the glorious man who walks through. This would be a whole lot easier on me if he was hideous. His good looks are blinding, and it takes me a moment to remember what a monster he truly is. Even if his faded blue jeans hug his hips in a way that makes my stomach twist, or if his shirt looks like it's glued to his perfect chest.

Fuck me.

What is wrong with me?

I should be afraid of this man. God knows he has made it clear what he'll do if I'm not.

He carries a tray in his hands and, without a word, he slams it on a nearby table and turns to leave. Oh, so he's not going to speak with me? The fucking man dirty danced with me at a club, drugged me, locked me in a room, and now he thinks he can just walk out? I don't think so.

A thought trickles into my mind as I open my mouth to speak. I read somewhere once that a captor avoids talking to a captive because they're always weary of creating any sort of bond, or even emotion. If there is even a shot at getting through to this man, I'm going to take it. Maybe it'll be fruitless, but I'm not about to sit back and do nothing.

"Jagger," I murmur, eyes fixated on the tattoo lining his back.

I'd take a wild guess and say it's a nickname, judging by the way he turns, eyes narrowed, staring at me as if I've called his name.

"How original," I mutter. "Great nickname."

His glare hardens and he crosses his arms across his chest, causing his muscles to jump and bunch. "It's of no use to you, either way."

"I should at least know who the bastard is who captured me, if I'm staying a while. Don't you think?" I smile sweetly.

His jaw tics. "The only thing you need to know about me is that if you continue smart mouthing me, I will tape your fuckin' lips closed."

I close my mouth, but only for a moment. "Are you this charming toward all women, or only the ones you kidnap?"

He grunts. "My life is none of your business."

I shove a finger into my chest. "My life is none of yours, either, but that hasn't stopped you."

He storms forward, and I keep my eyes fixed on his, challenging him. He stops in front of me, anger washing over his face. "I know what you're doing, and it won't work. Act tough, be brave and witty, but let me tell you this ... I will break you, little girl, because everyone has a weakness, even you."

Then he turns, walking out and slamming the door without another word. I stand, staring at the door for long moments. He's wrong—he won't break me because I won't let him. I stare at the tray of food and my stomach grumbles. I hesitantly go over, lifting the silver lid off the dish. There isn't much, but it's food, and I'm not about to starve to death on top of everything else. I pick up the ham sandwich and bite into it, chewing slowly.

I haven't eaten since before the club two nights ago, and my body isn't ready for the food that comes rolling in.

The second it reaches my stomach, it twists violently.

"God," I mutter, dropping the rest of the sandwich. "Fuck."

Praying I keep the contents of the food down, I climb into bed again and close my eyes, hand over my stomach until I fall into a fitful sleep, exhaustion getting the better of me.

~*~*~*~

I don't know how long I sleep, but I wake at the sound of the door opening. I sit up slowly, eyes blurred, and stare at the door and gasp as not just one, but five men enter the room. It's so shocking that it takes me a moment to convince myself I'm not dreaming.

I grip the blanket, pulling it close to my chest, and my heart thumps against my ribcage. What the hell are they here for? Maybe they have decided it's easier to get rid of me. I can't see Jagger, or Johnny, or whatever the hell he goes by, and that is more alarming than the five men in my room.

"Well would you look at that, Willow Barnes …"

I stare at the man who has spoken — he's tall, well built, and gorgeous with blonde hair and green eyes. In fact, they're all scarily attractive. Where did he get these guys? Military drop outs?

"Who are you?" I ask, keeping the blanket tucked to my chest.

"Get up," he orders.

Oh, I don't think so.

"No."

"I'll ask you once more, get up or I'll get you up."

"I don't fucking think so," I snap, even though my insides feel like they're turning to jelly.

Green eyes flaring, he storms toward the bed and hauls me up, forcing me to my feet. He slams me down so hard I lose my footing and topple backward, tripping and falling against a nearby coffee table.

My head slams against it, and I cry out as pain shoots through my temple. Pressing my hand to my head, I can see blood coating my fingers.

What the actual hell.

"You bastard," I snarl. "What the fuck is wrong with you?"

"You will learn very quickly you'll do as you're told around here. Now, get up and come over here or I'll break your fingers one by one until you do."

I stare at him, for long, long moments, but something in his cold gaze tells me he's not joking. I stand on wobbly legs and walk over, stopping in front of him but refusing to meet his eyes.

"Fast learner," he mutters.

"What do you want?" I grind out, but my voice is a whole lot less powerful than it was a few moments ago.

I keep my hand pressed to my head. I can't see how bad the wound is, but I don't want to get covered in blood.

"I want answers," he growls. "I want to know everything you know about your father."

"Here's what I know," I grind out, finally meeting his glare. "He's dead. Dickhead."

He raises his hand to slap me, but Johnny is in there and has his hand crushed in his grip in a split second. It's so fast it takes me a moment to register just how quickly he appeared. "Hit her once more, Snake, and I'll break your fuckin' fingers. What the fuck do you boys think you're doin' in here?"

"Gettin' answers," Snake grinds out. "This is takin' too long, Jagger. Do your job."

Jagger moves quickly, pulling a gun from his jeans and grabbing Snake by the neck, slamming him against the wall and pressing it to his neck. My eyes widen as I watch the man, who was so confident only minutes ago, turn pale as he's faced with the reality of having that cold steel right against his flesh.

"You doubtin' me?" Jagger snarls, baring his teeth in a way that makes him look terrifying.

"We need answers," Snake mutters, his voice hoarse.

"And we'll fuckin' get them when I say it's time to get them. You keep your hands off."

"She was bein' a smart ass, she deserved what she got."

"I don't give a fuck what she's doin', it ain't your place to be in here. She's my business. If I see you lay a fuckin' finger on her again, I'll gut you." Jagger drops the gun and shoves the man out of the way, and then he turns and stares at me, his eyes scanning over the blood on the hand that is still pressed against my head.

"Answer the question, girl."

"I did," I say, my voice weaker than I'd like. "I don't know a damned thing about my father."

"Tell me the name of the police officer that came and informed you of your father's death."

I close my eyes, trying to remember. I consider lying, but I know that won't benefit me. Whatever my father got himself into, he chose to leave Jenny and me behind to make sure he was protected for it. What about us? Did he even consider that we could be in danger? The man I thought was a hero turns out to be just a phony.

"Huck," I mumble, opening my eyes and staring at Jagger.

"Fuckin' knew it," one of the other guys mutters.

"What did they say happened to him?" Jagger goes on.

I swallow. Keep calm, just answer the questions and they'll leave. "He was in a car accident."

"Did you overhear Huck saying anything unusual, at any time?"

I close my eyes, trying to remember that time. I was devastated, trying to look after my sister and trying to stop my mother from killing herself in the first week.

There was once, though, because even through my hard time, I thought it was odd. I found Huck out back on the phone after he had come to ask my mother questions. He spent a whole lot of time asking her questions. Whoever he was talking to, it was very rapid.

"He was talking to a guy named Ben. He was telling him not to breathe a word of this," I say, repeating what I can recall. "Something about … if anyone finds out what is going on, we're all dead. Then he said something about Manchez and his gang doing anything to get information."

"Is that all?"

I nod, and he turns toward the other guys. "Angel, Ace, and Rusty, you three go out and find Huck. It's time we have a word."

Three of the men retreat with a sharp nod, and the other two remain, staring at me with hard expressions. It never occurred to me until now just what I am dealing with. These men are part of something very dangerous. They're dangerous. It's written all over them. Maybe I'm not as safe here as I would have liked to think.

"Leave," Jagger snaps, and the other two exit the room.

When they're gone, he turns to me. "Come with me."

We're leaving the room? He's letting me out? I follow him out the door and out into the massive house. It's big, but I already knew that. The room I'm in is nice, but when I look out the window I can see other parts of the house if I look hard enough. We walk into a massive kitchen, with marbled benches and chrome fittings. Jagger takes my shoulder and shoves me down onto a stool, opening the cupboards and coming back with a first-aid kit.

I don't dare say a word. If he's helping me, then maybe my plan just might work. If he actually begins to like me, maybe I have a chance here. He pulls out some swabs and begins wiping my cheek to remove the blood that has trickled down. Neither of us speak. He then moves on to the wound on my temple, washing it before putting a patch over it. Gripping my chin, he tilts my head back so the light shines down over my face. Then he releases me with a sharp nod and scoops up the swabs.

"Why is your nickname Jagger?" I ask, daring to take the risk.

He pauses midway through throwing them into the bin. It seems my question has stumped him. He drops the rest of them in and then looks over at me with narrowed eyes.

"Does it matter?"

"No, but I want to know …"

"It's just the name that we came up with. A brotherhood."

"Why did you pick that, though?"

"Why are you asking so many fuckin' questions?" he snaps.

"I think I'm allowed to ask a damned question considering you haven't asked me any, like the one where you asked me if I wanted to be here ..."

His jaw clenches and he gives me a hard look before muttering, "Johnny, Aiden, Greg, George, Eddie, and Rusty. Think you can figure out what that spells. Been together since we were kids, and it stuck. All the boys except Rusty go by created names, which is what you hear me call them - Angel, Ace, Bull, and Snake."

So they're basically a gang?

"You're a gang, then?"

"We're not a fuckin' gang. We're a brotherhood."

"Same thing," I say, tipping my head to the side. "You're like an MC without the motorbikes."

"Be very careful what comes out of your mouth next," he snips, his voice a warning.

I cross my arms, glancing around the house again. "Can I come out of that room?"

He's over at the sink now and he stops moving again at my question. Without turning, he says. "You will stay in there because I don't trust you."

"Please, you can supervise. I don't want to spend the next … however long … in that damned room. Surely you have some heart."

He spins around, slamming a glass down onto the bench. "This isn't a hotel, princess, you're not here to enjoy yourself. If the room isn't good enough for you, I have a dark basement riddled with rats that you might prefer?"

I grit my teeth. "Fine."

His eyes lock onto mine. "Trust me, we're not the only people looking for you. If Manchez and his gang got hold of you, that room would look like fuckin' paradise. You should think yourself lucky."

"Who is this Manchez anyway?" I ask.

"Manchez is the most feared gang leader in this city, and he wants the information your father has. You don't even realize the danger you were in, do you?"

"It would appear not," I mutter.

"As I said, think yourself lucky we got you."

"What about my sister?"

"She ain't his child. As far as anyone knows, you're the only one he cares about."

"How did I not know I was in danger if so many people are apparently after me?"

"It took a while to link back to him, but when we did, we figured out we weren't the only ones after what he knew."

Right.

That's just fan-fucking-tastic.

"Can I go back to my room? I'm done sharing life stories."

I push out of my chair and walk back into the room and over to the bed I'm starting to realize is going to become very familiar in the coming weeks. I turn and face Jagger as he begins to pull the door closed. "How long am I going to be here?"

His hard gaze locks onto mine before he closes the door. "However long it takes."

Then with that, he's gone.

God help me.

# 3

Your mind will do crazy things when it's left to just think. Five days, it has been five days since I've had human interaction. Whatever they're doing out there, they no longer need me for it. I get tossed food, water, and am given zero conversation. I've paced, I've sung, I've danced, I've cried, I've done everything in my power to try and keep my mind from going crazy, but with my genetics and history, that isn't going well.

It's on the morning of the sixth day that I decide I've had enough.

I've worked out the times to perfection, the times he comes in to drop off the food. I'm not spending another second in this hell hole; I'm getting out of here before him and his minions decide they no longer find me useful. What if they decide they can't release me back into the world now I know what I do? Will they make me disappear just as they have so many before me, I'm sure?

I can't let that happen.

My eyes zone in on the table where Jagger walks in and places my food trays. It's near the door, a little to the left. He basically just steps in and places it down before ducking back out. If I drag the table a little further away, he'll have to come into the room a bit more and when he does, I'll take my chance. You see, in the mornings Jagger is alone, I can tell by how quiet the house is, not to mention I watch all the trucks roll in after lunch. The guys come in, they do whatever it is they do, then they leave.

If I can take Jagger down, I can get out of this house.

It took me a while to unscrew the lamp from the table, the smart bastard made sure it was fixed. I spent hours looking for something I could manipulate the screw with and managed to find a small paper clip behind the old desk that works. It took me hours, god, so fucking long, but I managed to move the screw enough to get the lamp off with some force. I'm going to use it when he enters this room, and I'm going to go home.

My mind is consuming me. Eating me alive. I can't stay here any longer.

Lamp in hand, I wait by the door for Jagger to enter with my food.

Exactly the same as every other morning, the keypad beeps and the door clicks open.

He goes to place the tray down but realizes the table has been moved a little out of the way and the moment he does, he looks up and sees me, lamp in hand, a smile on my face.
"Surprise."

I hit him.

I don't want to kill the man, but I do want him to go down.

He does, with a growl and a bellow of pain, he stumbles backward and falls to the ground. I lunge for the door, slamming my hand in it just before it clicks closed. I push it open, lamp still in hand, heart racing, and stare down at Jagger. He's on the ground, dazed, hand over the bloodied wound on his head. Shit. He won't be down long. I drop the lamp, and I run. The problem is, I don't know where I'm running to.

I dart past the kitchen and toward what looks to be a living area. Usually near a living area is a front door. I'm right, and the moment I can see the large brown exit in my sights, my heart kicks up a notch. I just reach for the door handle when I'm hauled backward. Two big, strong arms go around my waist and pull me so hard I can practically taste my freedom being ripped from me.

Screaming, I do everything in my power to fight, but he's too strong. He drags me back toward my room, grunting as I fight. But oh, do I fight. I fight with everything in my power, kicking and clawing, screaming and thrashing, but I'm no match for the large, powerful man holding me. When we reach the door, I latch onto it, refusing to let go as he jerks, trying to pull me away so he can get to the keypad and open it.

"No," I scream. "No."

"Fuckin' let go," he bellows, jerking me backward so hard my fingers slip from the handle.

He spins me around and pins me to the wall with one forearm across my throat, holding me there as he uses his other arm to reach out and attempt to open the door.

I grab at his arm, pushing as I become a little dizzy from the pressure he's applying. "Let me go you filthy, rotten, disgusting human being."

He looks toward me, panting, blood running down his face. "Did you honestly think you'd fuckin' escape me?"

His voice is like a whip, low and dangerous.

"I will escape you," I growl, leaning in close to his face. "I will fucking escape you, and you'll never find me again."

"Best of luck with that."

"Don't put me back in there," I plead, my voice cracking now, my strength turning into a pathetic whimper. "Please, I'm begging you. I'm going crazy. You don't understand."

His eyes lock on mine, and the pressure releases just a touch from my throat.

"You serve no purpose for me except to gain information. I'm not here to make your stay good."

I have to do something.

Anything.

In my pathetic moment of need, I do something stupid. Something insane. Something that makes me feel and look even worse than I did before.

I lean forward and catch him off guard when I press my lips to his. For a moment, he stands stunned, not moving.

"I can give you something, something you want," I murmur against his mouth. "I can serve a purpose, if you need me to."

He growls, and when I kiss him again, he lets me. He lets me kiss him long and deep, and he responds. His lips are coated with the faint taste of blood and his mouth is hot, hungry, and fucking delicious. I kiss him and my body comes to life, the desperation in me turns to a need that I can no longer fight. There is probably a name for it, but I don't care. I just want something … anything.

His forearm releases from my throat and he hauls me against him, kissing me so hard my mouth burns, but oh, I don't care.

I need him.

Want him.

Fuck.

I need him inside me.

I need something else, anything other than what I've got.

"Take me," I plead against his lips, rubbing my body against his hardening cock.

With a growl, he hauls me up against him with a hand to my backside, grinding me against his long, hard length. Then his other hand slips beneath my clothes and into my panties. The moment his fingers glide over my clit, my legs begin to shake. I am so wound up, so full of an emotion I can't even name, that I know my body is going to respond quickly. Mouth consuming mine, he flicks my clit until I am on the edge of orgasm.

Then, he jerks his hand from my pants and shoves me against the wall, hard. My body being torn from him is a shock, but my orgasm being ripped from me is torture. He leans in close, eyes deadly. "Do you think I'm so fuckin' stupid that your little sexual advances will actually work? Nice try, sweetheart, but I have no interest in fucking you."

His words are like a blow to my very fragile mind.

"Your dick would say otherwise," I growl.

"I can torture you in ways you could never imagine, you so much as think about touching me again. What I just gave you, that was nothing on what I'll do if you so much as attempt escape again."

"That was torture?" I laugh, bitterly. "Please, I've had a better time touching myself. In fact, I don't need you to finish the job."

I slip my free hand into my panties and flick my clit, eyes never leaving his. He thinks he can play twisted games, oh, I can play them too. I rub, moaning as the pleasure quickly comes to the surface.

"Fuckin' stop," he growls, but he can't make me because if he does, he'll have to release me and he won't risk that.

"Yes," I breathe, rubbing, never taking my eyes off his. "Oh god."

I find my release with a whimper and a tremble that has a growl coming out of his throat that is guttural. With one, angry twist, he spins me around and slams my face into the wall, hand on the back of my head. I laugh, bitterly as he unlocks the door and then shoves me inside.

"Keep playing your games," he growls, "I can make your life a living hell."

With that, he slams the door.

Effectively locking me back in my prison once more.

He thinks he can play? He doesn't even know the start of it.

~*~*~*~

Another two days pass, but he doesn't come back. One of the other guys comes in and delivers my food and water, and he does so with a gun so very openly shown in the front waistband of his pants. I am beginning to feel claustrophobic in this room; it doesn't matter where I go or what I do, the walls are closing in around me. I'm ashamed of my actions, yet at the same time I know I stirred something within myself, a desire to fight, a desire to show Jagger that I'm not going to roll over and take all of this.

I have thought a great deal in the last few days about my family, my sister, my mother, Ava ... I wonder if my mother ever knew about what my father was doing. Did she know he was into bad business? Is that why she's so crazy? Does Jenny know? Are they looking for me? By now, they had to have alerted authorities that I'm missing, but will anyone believe them? Ava will fight, I know she will, she won't back down until she gets answers. I love her for that.

I think, also, about the man holding me. How can someone so beautiful be so tangled up in this dangerous world?

Is he truly a monster? Or does he just want me to think that?

As much as I hate him, I can't help but think about his lips on mine, his hands on me, and relish in just how good that felt. I'm certain my mind has gone and run off on me, because I'm actually fantasizing about my damned captor.

I'm ruined.

I'm sitting by the window. What time it is, I don't know. I stare desperately at the trees outside, just needing a single second to breathe in the cool, crisp air beneath them. I hear the door open and am surprised when I turn and see Jagger standing, holding a tray of food. He's dressed all in black, like he's about to go to someone's funeral. Heck, maybe he is. It's hard to tell anything when his face is always that same, stone cold, expressionless perfection that I can't read.

I want to slap myself for feeling any kind of attraction to this man. He's a god damned asshole and yet here I am, admiring his utter perfection. His rugged good looks make my insides flutter.

Whatever happened to personalities and all that? I blame my lifestyle. My mother wasn't exactly going to win mother, of the year and she never taught me anything about self respect and going for the nice men.

My father, well, he "died" before telling me the values I should be seeking.

I stare at my kidnapper. I think Jagger has a personality, it's just hidden behind his tough act. I wonder what he'd look like if he smiled?

Probably knock me off my damned feet.

"Food," he mutters, pointing to the tray. I snap out of my thoughts and stare at him, all caveman like and grunting.

Really? That's the best he's got after what happened the other day? I can't help but notice the swollen bump on his head, the wound scabbed over. I do feel a little bad, I could have killed him after all.

"Me caveman, you little woman … ugh ugh," I mutter, standing.

His eyes widen and a ghost of personality flickers in those depths, but he quickly smothers it. I think back to the club, and how he charmed me with his fake smile.

"Keep the singing down, you're drivin' me fuckin' crazy," he growls.

Oh, that. I have been making a point of singing as loud as I can during the night, knowing full well it'll send him over the edge. If he wants to lock me in a room, then he can sure as hell fucking deal with what I decide to dish out to him.

I shrug. "What would you do if a crazy man kept you captive in a small, horrible room?"

"I wouldn't be so stupid as to get caught."

Ouch.

"You drugged me, I hardly had a chance," I snap.

"Didn't your parents ever teach you not to take drinks from strangers?"

"My parents weren't the darling couple you assume. My father was always working, and I'm fairly certain it was because he couldn't handle my mother. They didn't have time to teach me anything. Not that it's any of your business."

Jagger leans against the door frame and stares at me, arms crossed. "I didn't assume anything."

"You assumed I'm stupid for taking the drink."

"I just assumed you would know better."

"Well excuse me for finding a man attractive. I thought I was going to have a wild passionate night with a gorgeous dude, instead I got kidnapped by a fucking crazy person."

He glowers at me, stepping forward. "Careful."

"Or what? What are you going to do, Jagger?" I challenge.

His face hardens. "Do you have any idea who you're dealing with?"

"I. Don't. Care."

He steps forward again, like a god damned lion stalking its prey, and I shuffle backward without thought. He smirks. I have learned Jagger's smirk is so far from a smile, it's deadly and dangerous, and he knows it.

"If you don't care, then why are you shuffling backward?"

"If you want to hurt me Jagger, just do it and get it over with. You're either a nice guy, or a bad guy, no one can be both."

He spins around and walks to the door, then turns and looks back at me. "Can't they?"

# 4

*"Willow, you can't keep doing this to yourself."*

*"Why not, Jenny? You tell me, what is there to live for? Tell me. Because right now, it seems like nothing but an endless spiral of darkness and pain."*

*"Life can be hard, and then it gets better. You just have to wait for those moments where it's better, I promise you, they're coming."*

*"You keep saying that, but I haven't seen them. I haven't even felt them."*

*"Maybe, but if you hurt yourself, one day there will be no coming back and you'll never have the chance to experience them."*

*I meet her eyes. "Maybe that's what I want."*

*She frowns and takes my hand. "It's not what you want, you're in a dark place but it will get better ..."*

"Get out of there, now!"

The pounding on the bathroom door snaps me out of my intrusive thoughts, thoughts that are consuming my mind now more than ever. It has been another two days, and I'm in the bathroom, soaking in the soap less tub, refusing to acknowledge him. They've given me the essentials, a bar of soap, a toothbrush and, occasionally, they bring me a tiny bottle of shampoo and conditioner. So showering is easy enough, but having a bath isn't. I decided today I was going to soak in the hot water, even if I didn't have any bubbles.

My mind needed it almost as much as I did.

Another bang slams against the door, making the entire room rattle.

God, someone is moody.

Huffing, I stand and climb out of the tub, wrapping a towel around myself and walking over, opening the bathroom door. Jagger is standing, arms crossed, fury tight on his handsome face. His gaze drops down to my wet skin and his jaw muscle jumps. Did my kidnapper have a peek? I clear my throat and Jagger looks up to meet my gaze. He smirks and leans against the door.

"Tryin' to get the smell out?"

Oh, he's in one of those moods is he? Well, I'm not.

"Fuck off."

His eyes widen and he loses the smirk. "You're cooking for me tonight, it's about time you started earning your keep."

"Earning my keep? You're joking, right? You haven't given me a choice thus far, and if I had one, I wouldn't be here. I don't owe you shit."

"It's simple, sweetheart," he growls, leaning in close, "you either stay in this room or you have the chance to come out and do something with yourself. What's it going to be?"

I'd be lying if I said my heart didn't jump at the chance to get out of this room. Not only does it open the door for me to chance another escape, but it also might help settle the tormenting thoughts swirling in my brain on a daily basis.

"Aren't you scared I might stab you?" I grin.

He chuckles, low. "Try your hardest. Even if you succeed, you'll never get more than five meters down the road and my men will have you. Then, sweetheart, you really will wish you were never born."

"Call me sweetheart again, I dare you," I warn, eyes narrowed.

"Hurry up and get dressed or I might just change my mind."

I turn and slam the door in his face, then quickly pull on my clothes. Every few days, they rotate my clothes, giving me some clean ones. I don't bother to ask who they belong to, but they are women's clothes so I assume one of their flings. I drag the old comb through my hair and then stare at myself in the mirror. My hair is dull and in need of some serious attention, and my eyes … they're bloodshot and tired. Yes, this place is certainly pushing my mental state to its limits.

I walk out into the room and see the door is wide open.

I hesitate, because as far as I know, this could be some sort of trap. Why would he let me out now? What's in it for him? Hesitantly, I walk out of the open door and into the large house. As I approach the kitchen, he's sitting at a bar stool, staring down at something. Is he reading? Seriously? What's wrong with this picture? Is this man completely off his rocker? Surely he is, either that or he's really testing me out right now.

That's fine, I won't try and escape tonight.

No, two can play at his little games.

I walk right past him and go to the fridge, opening it. I glance around at the contents, and pull out a tray of chicken. Luckily for him I can cook and, oh, I can do it well. I pull out mushrooms, onion, garlic, and tomato paste. I slam them down onto the bench right in front of him, and he ever so slowly lifts his gaze to stare at me. I hold that gaze, for a long, long moment before going back to my meal.

Chicken spaghetti. A childhood favorite of mine.

"Smells good," Jagger murmurs, when I begin to sauté the onion and garlic.

I narrow my eyes, staring at him. This must be a test. It has to be. He's not nice, and he's certainly not this casual. What is he up to?

"Thanks," I mutter.

"Do you cook all the time?"

I shrug. "I like cooking, but most of the time I like to do it by choice and not because some asshole kidnapped me and forced me to."

He snorts. "Touché."

"Tell me, Johnny, do you make it a habit to kidnap girls to get what you want?"

He flinches. Someone doesn't like being called Johnny; I make a mental note to throw that one in there more often. I slice the chicken and notice his eyes scanning over the blade. He's not nervous, is he? I fucking hope he is.

"No, you're the first," he finally answers.

"Well, don't I feel honored?"

"It could be worse …"

"Tell me how?" I mutter sarcastically.

"I could have raped you, let my gang rape you, beat you, starved you, the list goes on."

"Well, lucky me."

"I have no intention of hurting you, Willow, but your mouth is pushing me to my limits."

I glare at him. "You've hurt me, numerous times."

He growls, low. "You've given me little choice."

"There is always a choice, buddy. You're making the wrong ones."

"My life is not a fuckin' fairytale, at what point did you think it was?"

"Oh, believe me, I know it's no fairytale," I growl, throwing the chicken into the pan.

As much as it kills me to admit it, being out of that room is a refreshing change and one I'm really beginning to enjoy.

"Then why do you defy me so often?"

"Do you want me to fear you, Jagger? Is that what will get your juices flowing? Well, news check, buddy, I don't. I'm not going to let you or your little gang friends break me. I'm staying strong for myself, it isn't to challenge you. I want to come out the other side of this with my sanity."

He stares at me for long moments and my cheeks heat under his gaze. I curse my reaction and pray it just looks like the steam from the pan is making my skin flush.

"How old are you?"

I blink. "Excuse me?"

"I said, how old are you?"

"You know so much about me, but you don't know how old I am?"

"Didn't bother to check. Now answer the question."

"Twenty-two."

He ponders that, his eyes growing hooded and almost relaxed. "Anyone waiting back home for you?"

"What do you mean?"

"I mean, when you get out of here, will you go running back to your Prince Charming and have him attempt to hunt me down?"

I snort. "If there was, I wouldn't send him your way. Even I'm not that stupid."

He grins, eyes flashing in a way that makes my tummy do a backflip. "You're learning, but you didn't answer my question."

"No, Johnny, there isn't anyone. Men are overrated."

He doesn't flinch. Doesn't even show a smidge of emotion.

"Are you finished with the small talk now?" I ask, stirring the chicken. "I'm not in the habit of chatting to my kidnapper."

He smirks, and I look away. This man has split personalities, I'm damn sure of it. I boil some spaghetti on the stove and then serve up the meal. My stomach grumbles, because I haven't eaten something that looks this good since I've been here. I slide a plate toward Jagger, and his eyes move over it before looking up at me. "Not bad."

"Don't get used to it."

He ignores my scolding tone and takes a mouthful of food, his eyes flashing as he swallows it. He looks up at me, and I can see he's enjoying it. The intense expression on his face makes my already twisted mind go to a place I refuse to let it. A sexual place where he's giving me that look as he fucks me slowly.

God damn.

I need to go back to my room, right now.

"Are we done?" I ask, voice tight.

"Sit with me."

It's not a question, but a demand.

I stare at him, lips purses. "Why, dare I ask, would I ever want to do something like that?"

"It's simple, Willow. Sit with me and eat, or go back to your room and starve. The choice is yours."

Fucking. Men.

I take a plate and sit down beside him, taking a mouthful. It's so good, and it takes everything inside me not to moan with delight. I don't, but my god, I enjoy every second of it.

"What happened with your ex-boyfriend?"

Has this guy lost his god damned mind? Why is he asking me this? "What is it to you?"

"Just answer the damned question," he growls.

"He was an aggressive dick," I mutter.

He drops his fork, and I dare to peek up at him through my lashes.

"Fuckin' trash men," he mutters.

"Seriously? You're going to judge another man for laying his hands on a woman?"

He glares at me. "I'd never hit a woman I loved."

"No, but you'd take a woman from her home and her life to fulfill your own needs. It's no better, Jagger."

He's silent a moment, and his eyes are focused intently on mine. "As I said, I'd never hit a woman I loved. I'd never hit a woman if I didn't have a reason to."

"Oh, wow, what a hero," I snap, shoving my fork down.

I'm suddenly full.

I stand and pick up the plates, taking them to the sink. As I drop them into the soapy water, I stare down at the knife on the side of the sink, wondering if I could ever gain his trust enough to get hold of that and stab him with it? The thought of actually having to hurt someone makes a sickness deep inside me stir to life, and I shove it back down. I never want to be in the situation where I have to do something like that, but if it means I get out of here, I'll do whatever I have to.

Jagger might be standing here, saying he wouldn't hurt a woman, but I have no doubt in my mind if it comes down to it, he'll do whatever he has to, including hurting me.

"Go back to your room. I have business to take care of."

I turn and walk off without acknowledging him. I walk into my room and shove the door closed behind me. My bottom lip trembles, and I'm fighting with everything I can to keep it together, but I don't know how much more I can take.

I'm breaking.

Soon, I'll snap.

~*~*~*~

Two more long, dreadful weeks pass, and the routine is the same. I get up, spend all day in the room, go out at night and cook for Jagger, clean up, and then go back to my room. The hilarious thing is, I could have stabbed him so many times when preparing the meals, but I'm not ready for that yet. No, when I make my chance at escape, I need to ensure it's done properly. I need to catch him off guard and, to do that, I need to let him believe he's got me right where he needs me.

I think a lot about my dad during my days sitting in this god forsaken room. I wonder if he's truly alive, and if he is, has he given any indication of coming to save me? Will he risk his life to help me or will he leave me here to rot? Because, as far as I can tell, he's in no hurry to help his daughter. I've been here for close to a month now, maybe even more, and I haven't heard a single word about him since the first week.

Whatever is happening, they're keeping it under wraps.

I'm sitting in my room one afternoon just staring out the window when the door opens. Assuming it'll be Jagger, because it always is, I'm surprised when I see Snake staring at me, his evil eyes formed into tiny slits.

He's a horrible man, it's written all over him. Why Jagger would ever trust him is beyond me. Jagger might not be the one to hurt me, but oh, I can almost guarantee this son-of-a-bitch will.

"Get up," he orders, taking a step closer.

I shuffle back into the windowsill. He gives me the damned creeps.

"Excuse me?"

He steps closer, and I cross my arms, as if that'll protect me from anything. "Get up. We're fuckin' hungry, and you're going to go out there and cook for us."

"Where's Jagger?"

"Fuck Jagger, he'll be back soon."

My heart skips a beat, and my chest tightens. At least with Jagger here, the other men don't touch me, hell, I don't even see them. Only twice in the two weeks has he left me alone, but never with them. He just leaves me locked up and goes out for a day or I don't see him until the evening because he's busy. Either way, it's always him that comes in and never them.

"Get up and get out there, or I'll take my belt off and wrap it around that pretty ass. I'm sure you'd enjoy that, wouldn't you, princess?"

Is he high?

God. He looks high.

He looks like he's on something because the glazed look in his eyes terrifies me.

"In fact," he goes on, "take your shirt and pants off."

"What?" I say, my voice shaky as I stand, moving along the wall in an attempt to get away from him.

He steps forward quickly and grips my shoulder, his fingers digging firmly into my skin. I gasp and jerk, but it's no use, he's too strong. He pulls me closer, his hot breath against my face as he hisses, "Off. Now. Or I'll make you go naked."

"No," I hiss, trying to jerk my shoulder from his grips. "You sick fuck."

He only tightens his fingers.

"What did you say?"

"I said no, you fucking bastard."

Something flares in his eyes, and without thought, he grips his belt, and, keeping one hand curled around me, he undoes it and yanks it off. I try to scurry away but he pins me by the throat and shoves me face first onto the bed. He's wild and untamed, a monster. A pure, raw monster. I scream and thrash, but it's no use. Snake brings the belt down over my skin, and the first slap has me screaming in agony. He does it again, and then again, over and over until my screams turn to strangled sobs and my skin goes numb.

"You think I'm going to go easy on you?" Snake roars. "You do as you're fuckin' told around here, bitch. He might go soft on you, but I sure as hell won't."

"What the fuck!"

An angry voice can be heard behind me, and the sound of it has Snake releasing me. I keep my face pressed into the pillow, my sobs tearing through the room as a pain unlike anything I've ever felt travels through my body. My skin feels as though it's on fire, and my heart is racing so hard I'm scared it might just stop.

"Get the fuck out, Snake. Now."

The voice is familiar, Angel maybe. I'm not so sure.

Snake leans down close to my trembling body and hisses, "Pull your fuckin' shirt down and if you tell him about those marks, I'll be back, and next time, I won't stop."

"Get out," Angel growls, and the sounds of shuffling can be heard as he leaves the room.

I don't move. I'm too scared to move. The pain is too much.

I hear the two men leave, murmuring for me to come out when I'm ready. I glance at them as they walk out the door. Angel and Ace, maybe. I don't know. My vision is blurred and the pain in my back is out of this world. God damn them, god damn them all to hell. I can't do this anymore. I can't be here. This is hell, and I'm not going to spend another second living in it.

I'll go out and make his dinner.

And then I'll slit his damned throat.

I lie on the bed until the tears dry up and my body stops trembling, only then do I push up and go into the bathroom, lifting my shirt to glance at the horrific welts on my skin. I feel physically sick as I stare at them, the pain almost too much to bear. Little spots of blood have risen to the surface. The man unleashed on me, lost it like a god damned psycho.

I pull my shirt down and, with a determination I'm not certain I've ever had in my life, I walk out of the room and into the kitchen. I pass the men sitting in the living area and avoid the deadly eyes of the man who is so dangerous he scares me. I take out some ingredients and begin chopping, the pain so intense I can feel my head spinning as I do what that piece of devil shit asked.

"What's goin' on here?" Jagger asks, entering the room from the hall, his eyes going to me.

"Nothin', boss. She just offered to cook for us," Snake says, calmly.

He gives the men a look, then narrows his eyes and focuses back on me. I give him no expression, my soul is numb. I continue cooking, and when the men retreat downstairs for beers, I get an idea. Maybe my mind has had enough, or maybe I'm just on the verge of losing it, but I'm going to get the hell out of this place, and I'm going to make sure they can't follow me.

I go the cupboard where Jagger keeps the first-aid kit and dig around quickly through the medicine cabinet. Jagger has only gone for a second, and I know it won't be long before he returns. He knows I can't escape just yet, I'd have to run past all the men to get out the door, but that doesn't mean he'll leave me alone for long. I shuffle through a few bottles of pills, when I finally find what I'm after. A jar of laxatives.

A feeling of overwhelming strength washes over me.

I walk over to the simmering sauce on the stove and carefully crush each tablet up and put them in. The entire bottle. I take a tiny taste, to make sure it's not too obvious, but the delicious sauce I'm making to go with the chicken rules it out. I take a knife and tuck it into my pants just as Jagger enters the room again, beer in hand. His gaze finds mine, and once again, I don't change my expression even a touch.

I don't want to hurt Jagger, because out of them all, he has been the best to me, but I can't stay here any longer either. This pathetic lust I feel toward him is nothing more than some twisted version of Stockholm's syndrome, and I'm not risking letting my brain take me there. No, I'm going to make them wish they never met me.

Voices drifting up the stairs cause me to snap back to reality and I jerk, hurriedly finishing the meal. Dropping a bean onto the floor, I reach down for it and wince as the pain becomes almost unbearable. I stand upright and see Jagger in the kitchen, eyes on me. He reaches out, curling his fingers around my arm. "What's wrong?"

If he finds out that Snake hurt me, all hell will break loose and my plan will fail. I bite back my furious response as I jerk my arm from his. The motion causing pain to radiate through my body.

"My back is sore because I've been locked in a god damned room for fucking weeks."

He makes a sound of frustration at my snarky response but doesn't say anything further. If I look at him, he will see the way my lip is beginning to tremble. I'm breaking. I don't know how much more of this I can take. I need to go home. I take the plates of food to the table, and when I place Jagger's down in front of him, he pushes it away.

"I've eaten."

God dammit.

I won't cry. I won't.

"But thanks, I'll have it tomorrow," he murmurs, eyes fixed on my face.

Why does he have to look at me like that? With that beautiful expression? He's making it so damned hard for me to want to do this. I don't want to have to hurt him to escape, but I will. I'm so god damned fucked up. He has completely screwed my mind and I'm crumbling with every passing second.

The men all scoff the food, typical male style. Then about fifteen minutes later as I'm finishing the washing up, Angel grips his stomach and groans. Soon all the men are groaning and holding onto their stomachs with desperation. Jagger looks over at me and the rage in his eyes has me running out of pure fear. I rush out of the kitchen and, hearing his footsteps close behind mine, I know I'm not escaping this house right now. I run into his bathroom, slamming the door and locking it, before dropping to my knees and letting out a loud cry as the pain becomes too much.

"Open the fuckin' door, right now," Jagger roars, pounding his fists on the frail timber.

I slide out the knife, this is my only chance. Jagger kicks and shakes the door, but he can't open it. Well-built house. Cars begin roaring to life outside, and I know the men are making a break for it. I just locked myself in the only bathroom other than the one in my room, and they're all going to need one very soon. This is my chance. The only chance I'll get. Jagger is alone. It's just me and him.

And, for the first time, I have a weapon.

"Open the fuckin' door or I'll break it down," he barks, pounding his fists on it, over and over again.

I grip the knife in my hands. I can do this, I can. I just have to turn my mind off. He's a monster, he is. He kidnapped me and has kept me here for weeks on end. He's not a kind man, he's not the kind of man you change. Clenching my eyes shut, I push the door open and without though, shove the knife forward but he's too fast. He catches my hand and jerks me forward.

The struggle begins, I kick out and manage to get him to release my wrist. I wave the knife away, so he can't catch me again. We begin a battle of strength and even though he's stronger than me, I'm determined. I use every ounce of strength I have left to keep him from locking me down. I lash out, kicking him in the shins hard enough to have him jerking back with a roar. He doesn't release my arm and, instead, pulls me toward him. I lose my footing, he looses his footing, and before I know what's happening, we're falling and the knife in my hand glides perfectly into his stomach as we hit the ground.

The sound it makes as it plunges into his stomach is enough to make vomit rise into my throat. I make a rasping sound, but no sound wants to escape my open lips. I get off him, staring down as blood pools and begins to soak his shirt. His hand moves to the wound and he grips it, looking up at me with a mix of shock and pain. For a moment, just a moment, I hesitate. Everything inside of me is screaming to help him, but I can't. I have to run.

I have to go home.

With a hesitation in my heart that I must fight against, I leap over him and run out of the living room and down the stairs. I find a set of car keys on a table beside the door, and I grab them before rushing outside. My back hurts, my heart aches, and my adrenaline is enough to cripple me but I push on. I press the button on the keys over and over, with trembling fingers, but there are no lights to indicate a car unlocking. Panic grips me. I have minutes, if that, before he gets up and comes after me.

There is no car here.

I drop the keys on the dirt, and I turn and stare out into the darkness. I have to run, it's the best I can do.

The morning will help me out of this mess. If I find a driveway, I might be able to follow it until I reach a road.

Then, I can flag someone down. With a deep, shaky breath, I start running. The sound of the front door slamming has me picking up my pace, but I don't know where I'm going.

A fear I've never felt before rips through me and I run as fast and hard as my body can take, but it's just not enough. I'm being slowed down by trees and pure darkness. Before I can make it to a driveway, or a road, a hard body slams against my back and my body tumbles to the ground, face slamming into the dirt as his heavy weight locks me down. I scream, a mixture of pain and frustration, as the man on top of me growls in pure, raw anger.

I thrash and fight, but it's no use, he's too strong, and I'm too god damned tired.

"Let me go, please," I beg, as he pushes up to his feet, jerking me up with him.

"You fuckin' stupid girl," he whispers into my ear, "you'll regret that."

"Jagger, please."

"Do not say my fucking name," he roars, so loudly my knees give out from beneath me.

I'm broken.

So god damned broken.

"Get up," he barks, pulling me up. "Get up."

Using whatever strength it seems he has left, he hauls me to my feet. Pain shoots through my back, through the fresh wounds on my face, and I can't help the desperate sobs that escape my throat as he pushes me toward the house. The moment we reach the patio, he jerks my hands behind my back to cuff me.

"Stop," I wail, the pain too much. "Please, stop. Cuff me from the front, I beg you."

He hesitates, only for a second, before cuffing my hands at the front. Then he shoves my face into the wall and jerks up my shirt. I cry out as the fabric, which has stuck to my skin, is ripped off. Tears roll down my cheeks, the pain unbearable.

"Who the fuck did this?"

"I …"

"Tell me who the fuck did this or I swear to god, I'll lose my shit and fuckin' end you, woman," he roars into my ear.

"Snake," I whisper between sobs.

He slams a fist into the wall beside me, and I hear the sounds of his bones cracking as it connects with the brick. His fist landed only inches from my face. I hiccup and turn my head away, on the verge of crumbling completely. He yanks my shirt down and spins me around. I get a good look at him now and gasp. His shirt is soaked in blood and his skin is scarily pale.

"You need help," I croak, terrified of the outcome.

I didn't think this through.

If Jagger dies and I'm still here, I'll be left with Snake.

What the hell is wrong with me?

"Not fuckin' likely."

"You could die, Jagger."

"If I die," he rasps, leaning in close, "so do you. Should have thought of that."

I swallow and stare into his pale blue eyes. "Let me help you."

He looks like he might pass out, but his face doesn't waver.

"You. Tried. To. Fuckin'. Kill. Me."

"I tried to escape," I correct him, pathetically. "If you don't let me help you, you'll get sick and you could die. If that happens, all this was for nothing."

He glares at me and then jerks my body until we're walking back inside the house. He hauls me up the stairs with a strength that is incredible for someone in his condition. He takes me into the kitchen, not releasing me as he goes to a drawer and pulls out a gun. Then, he goes and collects the first-aid kit. He then turns to me, uncuffs my hands, and points the gun right at my head.

"You try one thing, I'll shoot you. I won't even fuckin' hesitate."

Then, he nods to the sofa, and I follow him, watching as he lies down, raising his shirt. When his stomach is exposed, I wince to myself. It doesn't look good, and the good parts of me, the parts deep down inside, has me feeling horrible about it. The wound on his stomach is seeping dark, red blood in slow, thick rivulets. I use his shirt to put some pressure on it while I clean the skin around it. He doesn't make a sound.

"I'm sorry," I dare to say.

He doesn't say a word, he just points the gun at my head and watches me work. I clean around the wound with some antiseptic, and then I dig through the kit to find a needle and thread. I tie the thread and prepare the needle. So much could go wrong, he could get an infection, anything, but I know a man like him will never go to a hospital unless he's on his death bed. I hold up the needle and glance at him. He nods and leans back, closing his eyes, but he doesn't lower that gun.

The first pull of the needle through his skin makes my stomach turn, and I fight back the urge to vomit. He winces and tenses, and I can see his jaw clenching—it hurts but he's never going to admit that. By the time I'm finished, I'm shaking all over and I know my skin is a deathly shade of gray. I place the needle down and then pour more antiseptic over the wound before covering it.

"You need to see someone about this; I'm sure you have a doctor you can use that works outside of a clinic. I know people like you always have someone on hand."

He nods.

Not a single word passes between us.

I don't know where to go from here.

~*~*~*~

"Before you go, lay down on the sofa, face down."

I've just finished cleaning up, and I'm no longer trying to hide how much pain I'm in. Every movement has a wince leaving my throat and I'm hobbling, just needing some kind of relief. My bed, a bullet to the brain, something along those lines.

I look up and narrow my eyes. "What. For?"

My words come out strained.

"Do you want an infection or do you want me to help you? Lay down, I'll clean your back up, then you can go."

Any other time I'd argue with him, but for right now, I don't have a single ounce of fight left. I walk over to the sofa and, with trembling fingers, I lift my shirt up and over my head, tossing it on the ground before lying down. The moment my face hits the pillow, tears well up in my eyes, and I fight back the sobs. Jagger shuffles around and then a moment later nudges my shoulder with his hand.

I turn my face and see he is handing me two pills.

"Take them, they're strong painkillers. Knock you out, but you'll get some rest. I'm taking them too."

I glance at him and narrow my eyes. As if I'm going to take anything this lunatic offers me. "No thanks," I mutter.

"For God's sake, they'll help. Here, I'll take yours and you can take mine if you're so damned worried."

He snatches the two pills out of my hand and throws them in his mouth, swallowing them dry. Then he hands me the other two. I am in a lot of pain. Hesitantly, I take the tablets and the glass of water he hands me. I put them in my mouth and swallow them down before shoving my face back into the pillow.

Jagger silently gets to work, cleaning my back. Every wince begins to fade as the pills kick in and I begin feeling light headed. Finally, though, I'm experiencing some relief. "They're mostly surface wounds, rolling around in the dirt didn't help. I've cleaned them up, they're goin' to be sore for a few days."

He throws my shirt at me, and I slowly push up, head spinning. I turn to face him, my entire body warm as the pills give me a sense of calm I haven't felt since I've been here.

I study the man sitting across from me, shirtless, blue eyes tired and yet so damned hard. I rake my gaze over every inch of him, and even like this, he's utter perfection.

"Why would you have someone like Snake on your team if he's such a dick?" I ask, crossing my legs as I pull my shirt back over my head.

"Snake has been loyal."

"That's it?" I mutter. "That's all you've got? Snake is loyal?"

"When you do what I do, loyalty is all you've got. He will suffer for what he did to you, though, don't doubt that."

I tip my head to the side. God, I'm high. So damned high. I blink a few times and, as if my body is moving without me asking it to, I find myself shuffling closer to Jagger. His expression of pure shock doesn't stop me as I push up until our faces almost touch. "Why are you like this?"

"Like what?" he murmurs, not pulling back.

"Like this. All of the things you do, the bad stuff, why?"

His eyes scan my face. "It's the only life I know."

"That's sad," I murmur.

"Why are you so close to me?"

I laugh, slurred and almost drunk sounding. "I don't know. Are these pills making you feel all … light?"

"Why do you think I gave them to you. They're the only thing that works."

"Are you in pain?" I ask.

He shakes his head.

"Jagger?"

"What, Willow?"

"Do you want to have sex with me?"

The words are coming out, and I can hear them, but I can't seem to stop them. My entire body is light, my soul isn't heavy, and god, I want the man sitting across from me. I want him so bad. Whatever this is, I have no doubt I'll feel regret in the morning, but for right now, oh, I'm more than ready to let him take me.

"No," he growls, "you're high."

"So?" I say, daring to reach up and put my hand on his chest.

He flinches, but he doesn't pull away.

"There is a name for this," he rasps, glancing down at my hand. "Stockholm's Syndrome."

I laugh, bitterly. "Well, I always did like labels."

"You need to stop."

I slide my hand down his chest, past his bandaged stomach, and to his groin. His cock is already hardening when I wrap my fingers around it and squeeze. Fuck. Yes.

"Why?" I breathe.

With a feral hiss, he moves quickly, pushing me down onto the sofa, his hard body coming down over mine.

His lips, barely millimeters from my own, flare back to bare his teeth. "You want to feel good? You think that'll make all of this go away?"

"Yes," I whisper.

His fingers go to my panties, running up the damp material, then he slips them beneath until he finds my waiting depths. I moan when he grazes my clit. I need this. God, I just need something. Anything.

"Please," I gasp as he begins to softly stroke, up and down, bringing to life the kind of pleasure I have long since forgotten.

"You think this will take away from what you are?" he growls, increasing the pressure, and I can feel an orgasm building.

"No," I gasp.

"You think that if I fuck you with my fingers—" he leans into my ear "—with my cock, that you'll feel better?"

"Yes," I plead, arching my back.

"You're nothing but a captive, pathetic and weak. Once I'm done with you, I'll never utter your name again."

His hate-filled words only spur me on, and the pleasure builds, so intensely I don't think I can take a second more of it.

He turns his hand, releasing my clit for only a second, as he pushes two fingers inside me, dragging them out slowly, before plunging them back in.

His thumb continues the torment on my clit and the pleasure is too much.

"You like it when I treat you like the pathetic, broken, damaged girl you are?" he barks, making me flinch.

"Yes," I cry out, as the pleasure rises to the surface.

I scream in release as an orgasm unlike anything I've ever experienced tears through my body. I convulse beneath him, head dropping back, eyes closing, everything inside of me feeling like it's being ripped out in the best possible way. Only when I stop shuddering does he pull his fingers from my depths and push back, looking down at me as my eyes flutter open and my head spins, a mix of pleasure and exhaustion.

"You're nothing, you'll always be nothing, and your body won't change that."

His words, scathing and broken, should hurt. They should but they don't, because it's true, after all.

I close my eyes as the drugs take me, and I can no longer find the energy to lift even a finger.

I'm nothing.

# 5

A few days have passed since Jagger and I had our encounter, and in that time, he hasn't come anywhere near me except to drag Snake into my room late one afternoon and beat the living shit out of him. Terrified, I watched on as he punched into the man, over and over, until he lay on the ground in a bloodied heap. Then, with empty eyes, he looked up at me and said, "Are you happy now?"

That was the last time I saw him.

I'm in the kitchen late one afternoon, doing what I do every day—baking. I have more freedom now. Jagger ensured every entrance to this house is guarded twenty-four-seven by men I don't know. He now lets me out of my room whenever I want, because he knows I can't go anywhere. Not only does he have men at the doors, but he has men at the gates and, as he so coldly informed me, at the end of the driveway.

Jagger has made sure I can't escape.

The television on the wall, that is small but runs all day, is playing a news story, and when my name is mentioned, I look up in shock.

My face flashes on the screen and a man can be seen, talking to a group of reporters outside of the bar I met Jagger the night he took me. "The search for Willow Barnes continues as family gathers together to desperately search for what happened to their loved one. Last seen on the evening of October twelfth, Willow is said to have left the club behind me with a man who is said to be in his early thirties, tall, well built, with blue eyes and dark hair. A search has been conducted, and many people have been interviewed, but so far, we haven't been able to find the missing woman. The police are urging anyone with information to come forward."

I stare with tears in my eyes at Ava and Jenny, both standing in the background, arms around each other, listening as the man talks. A pain builds in my chest, a pain I can barely control. They're fighting for me, looking, but they're not going to find me. Not yet, anyway. Not until Jagger makes a mistake. A mixture of pure raw emotion and relief floods me, because the knowledge that they're looking for me helps something inside of me. It gives me a strength I wasn't sure I had.

A soft sing-song voice has my head whipping around, and I furiously swipe my eyes as Jagger enters the room with a woman, a gorgeous young blond with huge boobs and a body to die for. He's half naked, wearing only a pair of unbuttoned jeans, jeans that dip so low I can see the dark trail of hair that begins running down. Swallowing, I meet his eyes and see him glancing at the television. It flicks off before the woman even has a chance to notice.

"Meet me in my room," he murmurs to the woman, leaning in and nipping at her neck. "I won't be long. I need to talk to my sister."

A pang of anger bursts in my stomach, and I clench my jaw as he walks closer, leaning a hip on the counter.

"You're taking a big risk bringing a woman in here. She could recognize me, you know?"

"She could, but considering she doesn't know my real name, or even how to get here, I think it's safe to say we're safe."

"Did you drug her, too?" I mutter.

"No." His eyes meet mine. "She was too busy sucking my cock to notice."

God damn him.

"You disgust me."

He grins, and oh, it does things to me, things deep inside that I'm fighting with every single ounce of strength I have left.

"I'll be busy for a few hours, the guys are downstairs. You know what happens if you try anything."

"You'll hunt me down and kill my family, yeah, I got it."

He leans in close. "Precisely."

"I hope you get fucking syphilis you piece of shit," I growl.

Even though Jagger goes easy on me most of the time, I have no doubt in my mind that if it came down to it, he would get hold of my sister to keep me here. I don't think he would hurt her, but I'd never let her be put in this situation. I feel so trapped some days, like I just can't get out. If I run, my family pays. If I don't, I suffer slowly in this hell hole. He is making it more and more clear that he's giving me no way out.

Growling, he leans in close. "Be very fucking careful what your next words are."

"Or what? What are you going to do?"

He moves quickly, hand curling around my neck as he backs me into the cupboard behind me, pressing me close and leaning in. With a low hiss, he tells me, "I've about had enough of you."

"The feeling is mutual," I spit back, holding his glare, not wavering even for a second.

He releases me and steps back. "Keep cooking, Willow. God knows it's all you have left."

With that, he turns and saunters off, leaving me standing, panting, furious. I look down at the knife on the bench and wish I had plunged it in a little deeper. I'm so tired of him, of this, of everything. Strength comes and goes, but depression is making a clear come back. Staring at the dull blade, I wonder what he'd do if I did sink its blade into myself. Would he let me die? Would he take me to a hospital?

The dark thought has my mind running.

Maybe I should test him, maybe I should see how he would react to walk out and find me in a pool of my own blood?

I know enough to know he isn't likely to let me die; if I had to guess, I'd say he would take me to a hospital. I could be wrong, though, and the risk really is equal parts, but if I don't do something, I'll just stand here, in this empty kitchen, baking a cake while he's in another room fucking some random woman. My choices are limited.

I grip the knife in my hand and swallow, staring down at the blade. Can I do it? Should I do it? Memories of the last time I brought a knife to my skin makes my stomach turn.

Do I have it in me to do that again? I press the blade to my wrist, just touching the skin there. Lightly.

The bedroom door opens and Jagger walks out, a towel wrapped around his waist. His eyes meet mine and he freezes.

For a moment, I see true shock in his face as his hands slowly come up in front of him.

"Put the knife down."

"Why?" I laugh, bitterly. "So you can keep me here and continue to torment me? Threaten my family? Take away every ounce of sanity I have left? What's wrong, Jagger? Don't want my blood on your hands."

"Put. It. Down."

He's scared.

For what, I don't know.

Probably the fact that he doesn't want to have to hide my body if I do this.

"Fuck. Put it down, now," he barks, stepping forward.

I press it harder. "Take another step closer and I swear to god I'll drag this blade through my skin."

"I'll fuckin' let you go, is that what you want to hear? The second we have your father, I give you my word that I'll let you go and never bother you or your sister again. I promise it will be over for you when this is finished with."

I look up at him and my bitter laugh breaks into an unexpected sob.

Broken.

I'm so damned broken. "You're a liar, a god damned liar. You won't let me go because I can ruin everything for you if I so much as open my mouth."

Blood trickles down my hand—I didn't realize I had broken the skin. Trembling, I stare at the red liquid, fear constricting my chest.

Jagger takes another hesitant step forward. "You have to trust my word."

Tears soak my face and my fingers tremble. He takes the opportunity to lunge at me, and soon my body is crumpling down against the cold floor and the knife skitters across the room. I fight him, with everything I have inside. I fight so hard it hurts. He grips my wrists and pins them above my head.

I struggle beneath him, my face soaked in tears. He lies on top of me, panting and staring into my pain-stricken eyes. I mumble incoherent words, over and over. He puts both my hands into one of his, and with his free hand he strokes tear-dampened hair away from my forehead.

Then, without warning, his lips are on mine. I didn't see this coming; I would have never seen this coming. I whimper and part my lips, and he slides his tongue into my mouth. I shouldn't want this, it's so wrong, and yet I can't bring myself to push him away. His lips are soft, luring me in and taking me over. His free hand tangles through my hair as he raises my head to deepen the kiss.

"Jagger?"

The female voice snaps us back into reality. He jerks his head up, not taking his eyes off my lips. I am panting, my chest rising and falling with want and desperate need. As if only just realizing what he has done, he shoves off me, his face tight, his breathing labored. He looks down at me, then back up at the woman standing, half naked, watching us.

"You said she was your sister," the woman says, her face scrunching in horror.

At any other time, this situation would be utterly hilarious.

"She's not. Don't leave. I'll be right back."

What?

What the hell is he doing?

Jagger reaches down and hauls me to my feet and then, without another word, drags me out of the room and back to my own. He shoves me in, his face so tight and emotionless it's terrifying. I take a shaky step back toward my bed, watching him. He looks to me. "You ever fuckin' do that again, I'll kill you myself."

With that, he slams the door closed.

What the hell just happened?

~*~*~*~

Jagger takes my freedom away.

For the next two days someone else feeds me and he keeps the room locked.

He's making sure I know where he stands.

He's making sure I know that what happened will never happen again.

He's reminding me I'm the prisoner here.

As the third day since I've seen him looms, I can feel something slowly creeping into my body. A sickness. It's hard to pinpoint, but it starts with a dull ache in my bones that quickly turns into a headache, and by the morning I'm so sick I can't move. Sweat coats my body as I wake from my slumber, and even though I'm soaked, I'm also freezing cold. Struggling to sit up, I push to my feet and slowly crumple to the floor, weak.

I need help.

I drag my body over to the door and begin slowly pounding on it, my broken, croaky voice barely loud enough to make a sound. It takes a few minutes, but eventually, the door opens and Jagger walks in, then stops dead when he sees me lying pitifully on the floor. His eyes narrow as they rake over me and he leans down, getting a better look.

"Are you sick?"

I open my mouth to answer him, but everything hurts so badly I can't form words. My mouth is dry, my head is pounding and my entire body feels as though I've been hit by a truck. I grip my head and groan, and, with a concerned expression, he leans down and places his hand against my forehead.

"Fuck," he mutters.

I groan again, and my world begins to spin. Jagger leans down and in one, swift movement, lifts me off the floor and places me down on the bed. He puts his hand on my head again and then turns and leaves the room. He's back a moment later with a cool cloth and some pain killers. I swallow them greedily, only to wince in pain when they slide down my raw throat.

"They'll help your fever."

"I need a doctor," I croak, rolling to my side, trying to relieve the pain.

"You know I can't do that. Get some rest, the painkillers will help, I'll be back shortly."

He leaves. The cold-hearted asshole leaves.

The painkillers don't work, and the shivering becomes so intense I can't stop the chattering of my teeth as I try desperately to get warm by pulling the big blanket over my body. By the time Jagger returns a few hours later, my bed is soaked in sweat and I'm drifting in and out of consciousness. The voices of Angel, Ace, and Snake can be heard as they chatter amongst themselves, but I'm only able to make out bits and pieces.

"If she dies, we could be in more trouble than it's worth," Ace says. "We've got to do somethin', boss."

"We can't take her to a hospital," Snake snaps. "If we take her to a hospital, we're done for."

"We can't let her fucking die either," Jagger growls. "There has to be an option here. Clearly she's fuckin' sick."

"Call your sister."

That's Angel.

Wait, Jagger has a sister?

"She'll flip if she knows we've been keeping a girl prisoner."

"It's the only option, Jagger. It's that or you take her to the hospital. The call is yours," Angel says, and then they all go quiet.

Or I pass out.

I must, because I'm woken to Jagger leaning on the bed, his hands on my face. My eyes flutter open and I stare up at him, vision blurry.

"My sister is coming, she's a doctor. You can't tell her why you're here. If you want me to help you, Willow, then you need to do as I'm asking. You tell her you're my girlfriend. You know what I'll do if you don't, so please … just tell her that."

He said please.

Maybe I am hallucinating.

I don't care what he tells her, I just want relief for this pain.

I nod weakly, and either I'm dreaming or he runs his hand over my forehead, pausing for a second, his thumb stroking over my skin.

I must be imagining things.

I close my eyes and exhale, just as the door opens and voices fill the room. A woman's voice stands out the most, and I open my eyes to see a beautiful woman with raven black hair, green eyes, and fair skin walking in. She's gorgeous, absolutely stunning. Not that I expected any less considering she's related to him.

She frowns, looking around the room, her eyes moving to the windows. "Why are the windows barred up?"

Jagger shrugs, casually. "I have things I don't want stolen from me in this house."

*Yeah like me.*

"She should be in a room with fresh air, Johnny. Some boyfriend you are."

Johnny.

I can't help but snort, even through my pain.

The woman walks over and looks down at me, swiping her hand across my forehead and then giving Jagger a stare that tells him she's less than impressed.

"Hi, Willow. My name is Maggie, and I'm a doctor. I'm going to figure out what's going on, okay?"

I nod, it's the best I can do.

Has she asked Jagger why he won't take me to a hospital?

Doesn't she recognize me from the news?

I don't understand.

"Can you tell me what's going on?"

"She's got fevers, shaking, her throat hurts, and she's been sick about four times." Jagger says, standing above her, arms crossed.

Maggie takes my temperature, checks my throat and vitals, and her face falls. "She's burning up badly, Johnny. Whatever she has, it's bad. Go and get my script book. I'll write something to help with the pain, fevers, and some antibiotics to kill any infections. Why didn't you take her to the doctor sooner?"

"It's a long way to drive. I thought it was just a cold."

She narrows her eyes, like she doesn't believe a word coming out of his mouth. "Well, you're lucky she didn't die. There are such things as a hospital …"

"The hospital wait times are long, you know that. Why would I go to a hospital when I've got a sister who is perfectly capable?"

He's smart.

Too smart.

She straightens and glares at him. "Next time your girl gets sick, Johnny, take her to a doctor. She needs some fresh air and a shower, she looks awful. My god, I know you were raised better than this. What is wrong with you? If I find out you're mistreating a woman …"

"He's helping me," I croak, interrupting them. "I was in trouble and only showed up yesterday. We have been seeing each other for a while, but I walked most of the way out here after a massive fight with my mother. I had no other way, and my phone was gone. I never got a chance to shower because I got so sick."

Maggie looks at me and Jagger actually looks entirely shocked.

"Well, it's not a wonder you're sick. Walking that far," Maggie says, her eyes still full of suspicion as Angel returns with her book.

She fills out a few scripts and hands them to Jagger. "Do not let her forget to take these, and if she doesn't get better within a few days, you need to take her to a hospital. Get her in the shower and open the damn window."

I like her.

His sister is something else.

I wonder, could she be my way out?

# 6

Everyone leaves the room and Angel tells Jagger he'll go into town and get what we need. Maggie leaves with Ace, the two of them talking, and when the door is closed, Jagger turns and looks to me. "Thanks."

Did he just thank me?

I'm so shocked, I just stare at him.

He moves without another word, toward the bathroom.

"What are you doing?" I whisper hoarsely.

"She's right, a shower will make you feel better."

He goes into the bathroom and begins filling the tub, then he leaves the room and comes back with some soaps and a washer. I watch him from the bed, still trembling and praying Angel gets back with the medication soon. My legs feel like jelly, and my body aches so bad I'm not certain I can actually get into that bath.

"Hate to break it to you," I croak. "But there is no way I can get in there on my own."

"Then I'll put you in," he murmurs, not looking at me as he scoops up a towel.

He's going to put me in?

Seriously?

I'm dreaming. This must be a dream.

"Can you get your clothes off, at least?" he asks.

I blink and slowly push out of the bed. With trembling fingers, I manage to get my clothes off and notice that the entire time, he keeps his back turned, not once looking at me. A pang of pressure in my chest makes me more than aware that this situation, with him, it's hurting me. It's getting to me more than I ever would have predicted. He passes the towel backward when I clear my throat, and I take it, wrapping it around me. My legs are wobbly and, as I take a step, I can't help but wince.

Jagger turns, stepping closer and scooping me up as if I weigh absolutely nothing.

I probably don't weigh much now, after over a month in here.

He puts my feet into the tub and then turns and lets the towel unravel, his hand holding onto it, and pulling it away when it drops. I slowly lower myself into the tub and oh, Maggie was right, this is heaven. I sink below the bubbles and close my eyes, forgetting the pain for just a second. Even the sting in my back doesn't hurt compared to the sickness consuming my body right now.

"Maggie, is she your only sister?" I ask, opening my eyes and looking up at Jagger, who is standing by the door, arms crossed over his chest.

"Yeah."

"She's nice."

He studies me. "Just finish your bath, Willow."

"Why are you helping me?"

His jaw tics, but he doesn't answer the question.

"You could just let me die, nobody would ever know."

"I'm not a fuckin' monster."

"Aren't you?" I whisper.

His eyes flash. "No, I'm not."

"You really believe that you're doing the right thing here, don't you?"

"No," he growls, "I'm doing what I have to do. Doesn't mean I like it."

I close my eyes. "You know, Jagger, in another world … I could have loved a man like you."

Silence.

Dead silence.

"Johnny?"

Maggie's voice fills the space and I open my eyes to see Jagger leaving. I can hear the two of them chatting outside the door, and a moment later, Maggie knocks. "It's just me, is it okay if I come in?"

"Yeah," I croak.

She walks in, her eyes going to my no doubt frail and pathetic body in the tub. She has a piece of paper in her hand and a few pills. "I have some pills you can take now, to help with the pain and fever. Angel will be back soon, this is a list of how many times a day you need to take everything."

"Thank you, I appreciate this."

She studies me. "You're sure everything is okay here? I know my brother can be bad news, but I'm not about him hurting women. You'd tell me if he was hurting you."

This is my chance, my chance to scream from the rooftops that I've been kidnapped, yet I find myself wanting to ask another burning question first. A question that has plagued me since the moment I came to this place.

"Do you know what your brother does?"

She swallows, looking away. "Yeah, I do. I don't agree with it, but him and those guys … it's all they've ever known."

"Why does he choose this life?"

She sighs and sits on the edge of the bath. "Johnny and I didn't have a good childhood. He got abused by our father and our mother killed herself when he was only four. I guess these guys, what he does, it's his way of having some sort of control over his life. He was always running off the rails and causing problems. Johnny isn't a bad person at heart, he can be gentle and kind, he's just got his priorities all wrong."

"What are you two doing in there?" Jagger barks, walking into the room.

"God, someone is pissy today," Maggie mutters, standing. "Chill, brother, I was explaining her medication."

"I've got to get her out now, I'll meet you in the living area when we're done. Angel just changed the sheets and opened the windows."

"Ah good, he's stopped worrying about his possessions and started worrying about his girlfriend," Maggie slaps Jagger on the shoulder and leaves the room.

Oh, if only she knew the truth. Jagger wordlessly helps me out of the bath and then turns so I can get dressed. It's a little easier this time, now my body is warm and the medication Maggie gave me is beginning to work. I walk past him when I'm done and go right over to the bed, with its clean sheets, and slide in.

"I'll come back in the morning to check on her," Maggie says, closing half the curtains but leaving some fresh air to come in.

"Thanks, Mags," Jagger murmurs, his eyes going to his sister for a second before meeting mine.

"Do better, brother."

He nods, and she smiles at me before leaving. When she's gone, I close my eyes. The bed dips and I know Jagger is sitting on the edge of it. I try to ignore the way my stomach fills with tiny butterflies. He's right about me, I have some sort of twisted captive obsession with him, and it needs to stop. It's not real. The things I feel are not real.

"How come she didn't know who I was?" I murmur, keeping my eyes closed.

"Maggie doesn't watch television often, she's the kind of person who just lives in a world where she prefers to know nothing bad. She's always been the same. But she will see it, I have no doubt about that."

"What will you do then?"

I open my eyes and look at him.

"I'll deal with it. Why didn't you tell her, you had every chance?"

"What's the point?" I mutter, letting my eyes fall closed. "You've made it clear what will happen if I do. I'm tired of fighting. I want to go home, and I just want this to be over and done with."

Jagger doesn't say another word.

The bed moves as he gets up, and then the door softly closes and I'm left alone once more.

For the millionth time.

I wonder which time it'll be that breaks me?

~*~*~*~

It takes two full days of sleeping for me to get better. Finally, on the third day, I'm able to get up and my body doesn't feel like it's giving way on me. The last forty-eight hours are a blur, and I remember very little of it. What I do know is that now, my door is open, and I'm desperate to breathe in the air of the outside world. I know there are guards, but I just want to stand outside, just for a moment.

I walk out into the living area and the entire house is quiet. Jagger must be sleeping, and the guys must not be here. I shuffle toward the front door and am surprised to see it isn't guarded. Heart racing, I twist the handle and step outside. I'm not about to run away, no, I just want a moment to breathe in the fresh air. I step onto the porch and see it's raining out, not heavily, just enough that a cool breeze trickles through and the soft sound of raindrops hit the roof. It's perfection.

"You need to get inside, right now."

I turn and see a guard standing on the porch, his eyes on me, one hand on the gun in his belt.

"Calm down," I mutter. "I'm not leaving, I just want some fresh air. Call Jagger if you need."

I step off the porch, slowly moving down the front steps, and then I step out into the rain, close my eyes, tip my head back and let the droplets fall onto my skin. Probably not the best idea considering how sick I was just days ago, but I need this more than I need my next breath and oh, as the water soaks into my skin, I feel the world calming down around me for the first time in a long time.

"I warned her to get back inside," the guard's voice murmurs.

"It's fine, thanks, Mick."

Jagger's voice is sleepy, groggy and god damned sexy but I don't open my eyes. I keep them closed, my head tipped back, soaking in every second of this perfection.

"You do know you just got past bein' very fuckin' sick right?" Jagger mutters.

I lean forward and let my eyes open and I see him, wearing nothing but a pair of gray sweats, standing on the front porch, shoulder against the pole watching me.

"I know," I say. "But I need this."

I stand for a moment longer and then turn, walking back up onto the porch. I go over to the old, creaky chair that looks as though it hasn't been sat in for quite some time, and sink into it, exhaling with relief and delight.

"It's fine, Mick. I've got it from here," Jagger tells the guard, and he nods before disappearing inside.

"Can I ask you something?" I say, meeting his gaze.

"Depends on what it is."

"How did my dad end up in so much trouble?"

Jagger looks taken aback by my question and, for a moment, he just stands there, arms crossed. Then, he pushes off the railing and sits down in a chair across from me. I try to keep my eyes off his body, the perfect definition in his abs, the way his biceps bulge and do not get me started on those gray sweats and the things they do for his cock. No, this sick, twisted obsession has to stop.

"Started with drugs, always starts with drugs. He was a cop, you know that, and he went undercover to bust a massive drug ring. He worked with the people I work with, and we trusted him. He became one of us in an attempt to destroy every last one of us. He has information, information that could do just that. We're not the only people who want that information. He went into hiding, protection, whatever the fuck you want to call it and well, here we are."

"It was his job," I say, crossing my arms. "If you don't want to go down for doing illegal shit, then don't do illegal shit."

"It wasn't just about the job, he was part of this, of us. We trusted him. Look, I stay away from the cops, they do what they have to do, and I respect that but he took the risk by going undercover and forming bonds with those men. He took an even bigger risk taking that information with him when he went into hiding, because he could have given it to the cops and he didn't. He has a plan, and I need to know what that plan is."

"And when you find him?"

Jagger's eyes zero in on me. "It depends if he's willing to work with us or against us."

"If it's against you?"

"He made his choices, Willow."

"So you'll end him, just like that?"

His face hardens. "If I have to."

I shake my head. "You know, you stand here and talk about what he did wrong, but look at you, look at your faults. You're no better."

"I never said I was," he growls.

"He mattered to me," I say. "In my screwed up world, he mattered."

Jagger stares down at his clenched fists. "If you mattered, he wouldn't have risked so much. If you mattered, he wouldn't have run and left you with your sick mother. If you mattered, he wouldn't have forgiven your mother for cheating on him."

"You're wrong, you know. We did matter. He ran to protect us. He didn't leave my mother because he loved me, because he loved Jenny. He took a child on that wasn't even his, and he gave her the kind of love she could have only ever dreamed of. You tell me another man willing to go to those lengths after being hurt."

Before he can answer, three trucks come rolling into the drive, and I watch as all the men get out. I study them as they walk closer, truly taking a moment to admire their utter beauty. Angel, being the tallest of the group , has this long, thick dark hair and the bluest eyes. His skin is creamy and that makes his tattoos stand out. He's well built and has the kind of coldness in his eyes that could be terrifying, but it also gives you an intense need to want to melt it to see what's beneath.

Ace is shorter than Angel, but equally as gorgeous. He has dark hair, messy and unruly, a few inches long. His eyes, the color of deep warm chocolate, are kinder than the rest of the groups'. He's thicker in build, his muscles strong and large. He has less tattoos, but truly, it makes him look even better.

Bull is the scariest of the group outside of Snake. He has this empty expression on his beautifully broken face. His hair is cropped short and is light brown in color. His eyes are a dazzling steel gray and his body is on the leaner side but strong and covered in tattoos. From head to toe, including his neck, he's all ink.

Rusty is an all American handsome guy, with long blond hair he keeps tied in a ponytail. He has a big smile, dimples and all, and the lightest green eyes. If it wasn't for the muscles, ink and bad boy complex, you'd pin him as the typical boy next door, though I have no doubt he's anything but.

As they stop at the steps, Snake gives me a truly terrifying look. I don't waver. I don't flinch. I glare right back at him.

"Lookin' better," Angel says, crossing his arms, his eyes scanning over me.

"I am."

"We have issues to discuss, boss," Ace says, nodding at Jagger.

"Right." Jagger stands and looks down at me. "Inside."

"No, I'll stay here."

"Inside," he grinds out. "It wasn't a fuckin' choice."

With a huff, I stand and turn, walking inside the house and into the kitchen. Fucking men. Fucking rude, asshole, men. They stay downstairs for quite some time and the thudding sounds coming from that general direction have my curiosity burning.

A quick look won't hurt, right?

# 7

I slowly make my way downstairs, tiptoeing as I do.

I don't want to get caught, but I'm very curious as to what the sounds coming from down there are from. The grunting and slamming have me concerned.

I reach the door to the basement and with trembling fingers, I push the door open. A small squeak is hidden by the grunting sounds that are now a lot louder. I sneak in, one step at a time, and when I get to the bottom of the stairs, I peer around and what I see has my entire body tensing.

Everyone is in here, all of the guys, and they're standing around a man who is tied to a chair, his face dripping with blood, his head slumped forward and there, standing in front of him, is Jagger. He has a knife to the man's throat and is barking something, something I can't make out because the buzzing in my ears is so loud it's all I can hear.

I watch in horror as Jagger barks another question, and the man doesn't answer. Jagger loses his cool and, with an angry movement, slides the knife across the mans throat, making blood spurt out in a way I didn't know blood could.

My mouth opens, but it's not until I see Angel lunging toward me that I realize I'm screaming.

Horror washes over my body as I realize the man who has held me captive really is the monster he's promised to be.

"Let me go," I yell, squirming in Angel's grips.

"You can't be in here," he grunts, hanging on tightly.

"What the fuck is she doing in here?" Jagger roars.

"I told you she should be fucking locked up!" Snake snarls.

"What are you doing down here?" Jagger barks in my direction, knife in his hand, blood dripping from it.

Oh my god, I'm going to be sick.

"She's fucking seeing shit she shouldn't see, fucking lock her up, Jagger, or I will," Snake warns.

Jagger turns and, without warning, slams his fist into Snake's mouth. The man stumbles backward, and I stop fighting Angel to stare in utter horror as he falls onto the ground and into a pool of the dead man's blood.

"If you fuckin' order me around once more, Snake, I'll fuckin' kill you," Jagger seethes.

"You're fuckin' weak, Jagger," Snake bellows from the ground. "She's made you fuckin' weak. You're not fit to lead us any longer. She's nothin' but a waste of space. I'll gut her with my bare fuckin' hands and get her outta the way so we can get on with it – she's clouding your judgement."

Snake's eyes zone in on me and I stare in horror, my entire body numb, as he pushes to his feet and reaches into his pants to pull out a gun. The entire world feels as though it stops and for just a second, I'm convinced this is it for me. That this is the end. I stare at the man whose cold eyes have promised horrible things since the moment I got here.

I can't even form words.

He's going to kill me.

As if in slow motion, Jagger moves, and the knife in his hand plunges into Snake's chest without second thought. It disappears as if the act didn't take any effort at all, but the way Jagger's jaw clenches and his arms flex, tells me it took more effort than I'll ever understand. The gun falls from Snake's hand and he drops to his knees, his eyes never leaving mine as he falls forward, his lifeless body slamming into the concrete floor.

"Let me go," I gasp, my entire body trembling.

"Can't do that," Angel mutters.

"Let me go," I scream so loudly the man behind me jerks.

Jagger nods, short and sharp, and Angel lets me go. I turn, and I run. I run as fast as my legs can carry me. I trip three times on the stairs, tears rolling down my cheeks as the images of what just happened play over and over again in my mind. Jagger just killed two people. Two human beings. As if they were nothing more than tiny frail animals. He didn't even hesitate.

He's a monster.

I reach the room and slam the door behind me, before running into the bathroom and locking the door, dropping to my knees and letting my head fall forward as sobs wrack my entire body. I can't make them stop. I'm not sure I even want them to.

I hear the door to the room open, and then a few seconds later the pounding of a fist and Jagger's roaring voice demanding that I open the door. I don't move. I don't even breathe. More pounding, and then a bigger sound, a larger sound. He's kicking the door. A few kicks later and the door flies open and Jagger steps in. I lift my tear-soaked face and see him standing, staring down at me. He's covered in blood, and I flinch away when he reaches for me.

"Don't touch me."

His jaw tightens. "You shouldn't have been down here."

"You … you … you just killed that man. You killed him. You just … killed him. And then Snake …"

"That man is a sick fuckin' rapist and part of the gang that could have taken you, but didn't. That man was looking for you, and would have had no problems in raping you while they figured out what to do with you. As for Snake, he lost his place, and with that, means you lose your place in this world, too."

"You're a monster," I whisper, pushing to my feet. "You need to let me go. Let me leave. I can't be here anymore."

I try to shove past him, but he grips me and pulls me against him, his arms so tight I can barely move. Blood smears over my arms and body, and I lose it, it's just too much. I start hitting him, punching him over and over with my tiny fists. He releases me, shocked, and I turn and practically dive into the shower, turning it on, fully clothed, needing to get this blood off. Blood from a dead man. Blood. Oh god.

Jagger is behind me in seconds, swinging the door of the shower open, stepping in.

He grips my arms and tries to pull me out, his voice rough as he attempts to stop my frantic scrubbing.

I scream and kick, cursing and swearing. I tear my clothes off, needing the blood away from my skin.

I don't care that I'm naked. I don't care. He continues trying to stop me, and I continue to slap him, hit him, punch him, kick him, and anything else I can manage – it doesn't stop him. He's soaked now, and his jeans hang limply on his large body. All the blood slowly washes off his skin and is sliding down the drain. He pulls me close, his eyes wild and flaring.

"Stop it."

"Let me go!" I cry. "Just let me leave, Jagger."

"Calm down, just calm down. You shouldn't have seen that. You shouldn't have been down there."

"Let me go, you're a god damned monster. Get off me. Get away."

"I won't hurt you, Willow."

"You killed that man."

"That man is a god damned monster, and so was Snake. You know that. You fuckin' know that."

"Let me go!"

I hit him again and he takes my fist, crushing it against his chest. He grips my chin in his free hand, and I struggle to get out of his grip.

Then his mouth is on mine. Without warning. Without hesitation. His lips are hot from the water, and he tastes terrifyingly good.

I should fight, I want to fight, but everything inside me forgets how to be rational. I can't fight this, desperation takes over and my body goes limp. He wraps a big arm around my waist and crushes me closer to his chest.

He parts my lips with his tongue, and I whimper when it contacts mine. Jagger is a man that can kiss, and when he does, it's wild and raw, avoidant of any emotion. He pushes me against the tiled wall, and I whimper when I feel his throbbing cock press into my stomach. I want him. It's so wrong, so disturbing, I shouldn't, but God, I want him. I run my hands over his bare chest, it's hard and firm beneath my palms, pure muscle. Raw, unfiltered male. When I slide my hands down his stomach and grip his jeans, he lets off a ragged groan. He's not stopping me.

He wants this.

In his own twisted way, he wants this just as much as I do.

I unbutton them, not moving my lips from his. He tangles a hand into my hair, and then slowly leans down to slide his lips across my neck, nipping the bare flesh as he does. He drags them down lower, until he reaches my nipple, he draws it into his mouth and groans when it hardens beneath his lips. Whimpering, I let my head fall back as he works my nipples over until I'm gasping and begging. When he stands back up, I grip his jeans and yank them down.

I stare down at the hard, thick length of his cock and my eyes widen when I see the four piercings in the head. God damn, that's terrifying and sexy. I look back up to meet his gaze and he's staring down at me with an amused expression. Tentatively, I reach out and take his length into my hand. He growls as I slide my hand over his shaft, gliding it up and down. Reaching down, he hauls me up until my legs are around his hips, and then he slides his hand between us, finding my clit.

Neither of us dares to speak. I know if I speak this will become real and this being real is a dangerous thing. Jagger is dangerous for me, and this situation is ugly but mostly, it's toxic. I have lost my mind, my control, my sanity, and I don't need to be reminded of that right now. When I feel myself heating from the inside out, as an orgasm nears, I clutch Jagger and cry out. He strokes me until he has managed to take every last shudder from my body.

Then his cock is probing my entrance and his lips are on mine again, furious and hot, kissing me in a way I'll never forget. When he lowers me over his dick, he lets out a guttural moan. I cry out as I feel him sliding inside me, stretching and filling until he is fully sheathed and growling. When he slides back out, I realize what the piercings are for. They hit the spot, right where they're needed, and oh, it feels incredible.

"Jagger," I whimper.

"So fuckin' tight, so fuckin' wet. I want you, Willow. I want you so fuckin' much it hurts."

It's only then I realize he has no condom on. I freeze and pull back, meeting his gaze.

"Protection ..."

"I'm clean."

"But ..."

"I got checked last month. I'm clean. Are you?"

I nod, biting my lip as he slowly slides back inside me.

"What about birth control?"

I nod again.

I've had an IUD in for quite some time now.

"Why now?" I whimper when he thrusts his hips, filling me so deeply. "Why do you want me now?"

"Because you make me fuckin' crazy in a way no one ever has before, and I can't fight it for a god damned second longer."

He drags his cock out and plunges it back inside me, making my whimpers turn to deep, pleasure-filled moans.

"Jagger," I gasp.

"You're so fuckin' tight. You're goin' to make me cum before I finish you."

He's filthy.

It turns me on in a way I've never been turned on before.

He thrusts his hips slowly, dragging his cock in and out with expert precision, finding that spot every time. My release is building and, oh, it feels so good. I grip his shoulders and slide my nails across his skin, tearing into the tanned, beautiful flesh. He thrusts harder now, and I can hear our skin slapping together as we both race toward release. He's groaning and he looks so erotic with his head tipped back, his jaw tight, the look in his eyes feral and untamed.

I can't hold back.

"Jagger!" I bellow his name as the best orgasm of my life consumes my body.

I arch my back and he reaches down, taking my hips into his hands and thrusting into me so hard I only scream louder. He leans down and bites one of my nipples, causing me to shudder and spasm around him once more. His fingers bite into my skin as he thrusts with desperation, searching for his own release. When he finds it, he groans, and I can feel him pulsing hot and deep inside me. His chest is straining, his biceps bulging. All I can think about is how utterly beautiful he looks right now.

When we come down from our high, he lets me slide off his hips. I wobble a little, and he reaches out to steady me.

When I dare to look at him, I get an eye full of pure, raw male.

He is panting, and his beautiful chest is rising and falling heavily with each breath.

His cheeks are beautifully flushed and his black hair is sticking to his forehead. Emotion passes between us, lots of it, and I wonder what he's thinking right now? I can't let the thoughts in, not yet. I'm not ready.

"Jagger!"

The loud booming voice outside of the room snaps us from our moment. Reality comes smashing back in, not staying away for long. Snake is dead. That other man is dead. We just had sex as if the world stopped. A crushing feeling grips my chest, and I look at the man in front of him, his face going from relaxed to tight in a matter of seconds.

"Fuck," he snarls, getting out of the shower and drying his hair. He jerks his soaked jeans on, even though there is no point. I stare at the faint red stains in them and my heart begins pounding beneath my ribcage. I know whose blood is on Jagger's jeans. He pulls them back on anyway, and takes the towel with him. He tosses me a towel and whispers at me to get behind the door.

He opens it and I hear him muttering, "She was tryin' to kill herself, again. What's up? Did you deal with the body?"

Kill myself? How dare he speak about me like that after what we just did? Who the hell does he think he is? Did he just use me as if I'm nothing more than a piece of meat?

He must have because he was never going to admit what we just did, instead he thought it best to say I was trying to kill myself. Pain consumes my body and grips my heart, and I feel my emotions shutting down.

When he's done, he turns and faces me. Without thought, I reach out and slap him. He takes two steps back, gripping his cheek, his eyes wide with shock.

"What the fuck?"

"Kill myself? Kill myself? That's your god damned reason for being in here? Fuck you, Jagger!"

He growls and pushes me against the wall, big hands on my shoulders. "A lot happened today, I don't need to be addin' to it by telling them I just fucked the captive."

Fucked. The. Captive.

"Go. To. Hell," I whisper, my voice barely audible.

"Willow, you're overreacting and you need to stop. You hear me, stop."

"You just had sex with me, and I thought ... I thought ..."

"You thought what?" he asks, his eyes scanning my face as if I'm some pitiful, broken, pathetic human. "That it changed anything?"

His words feel like a slap to the face. I can't even form words, my soul is crushed.

He releases me. "It can't happen again. You know that. It was a moment of weakness."

"So it was nothing? Just a moment where you thought, hell, I might just fuck the poor girl I've taken from her life for fun?"

"Willow …"

"Nothing, Jagger. I got it. Now get the fuck out."

He steps back and gives me a long stare before turning and slamming the door so loudly the window shakes.

~*~*~*~

When Jagger leaves, I go in search of alcohol.

I need something to shut my mind down, to turn off the thoughts consuming me. The fact that he just had sex with me — the most mind-blowing of my life — and then told me it meant nothing feels like a knife to the chest. It's not because I thought we were anything more than what we are, but because of the fact that I honestly expected my captor to give a shit about me. I've truly lost my mind, in a way that I can't come back from if I don't do something soon.

I find a bottle of vodka and unscrew the lid, sitting on the couch and drinking it down. The liquid burns, but I keep pushing, until my mind is numb and my body is warm. Then, I reach for the remote and turn on the television, needing something to distract myself, something to take away from the pathetic feelings swirling around inside me. I settle on Texas chainsaw massacre, finding the movie pathetically entertaining.

I watch as people are brutally murdered on the screen, and yet I can't do anything but laugh hysterically as they so pathetically try to escape.

"Run, idiot," I yell, waving my bottle of vodka around as yet another person is taken down by that chainsaw. "God, surely you're not that stupid."

A wicked laugh escapes my throat, and I shake my head in frustration and amusement as the alcohol briefly takes away the feelings of pain I'm harboring inside.

"You're dark and twisted, little girl, but your laugh is like sunshine."

Confused, and sure I'm hearing things, I turn and see Jagger standing at the entrance, staring at me. He has a bottle of whiskey in his hand, and he's drunk, so damned drunk. I guess he just went and did the same thing I chose to do. It's the first time he's not looking at me with that hard expression, the one he refuses to let me see past. Instead, his eyes are soft and glassy, his body is relaxed, and the bottle hangs effortlessly from his fingertips.

"I am not dark and twisted," I mutter, turning and facing the television once more.

"I could hear you laughing as soon as I came into the house. I assumed you would be watching a comedy, not a story about a mass murderer."

"Well, I happen to find it entertaining."

He walks in closer, bringing the bottle of whisky to his lips and staring at me. "Dark and twisted."

"Whatever you say," I mumble, bringing the vodka to my lips.

"Didn't know you drank," he mutters.

"Well, after today, it was the only thing I could think of doing. I see you had the same thought."

He nods, sitting down beside me on the couch, leaning back, placing the bottle in his lap.

"What, you're going to act like we're friends now?" I huff, shuffling away from him.

"What do you think, Willow, if we met under different circumstances, do you think we'd get along?" he asks, randomly, his voice slightly slurred.

He's as drunk as I am.

He wouldn't be here having this conversation if he wasn't.

"I suppose," I shrug.

"Why?"

I look at him. "Dark and twisted."

He grunts and the smallest grin appears on his face, making my heart do a stupid little flip flop. "That's a first for me, getting along with someone because we're both dark and twisted."

"Well, you're here with all your dark and twisted friends, I don't think it's that far-fetched."

"Hmmm," he murmurs, leaning back and closing his eyes.

"Why did you fuck me, Jagger?" I ask, boldly, staring at him.

He doesn't move, he doesn't open his eyes, he just lies there, head back, breathing deeply. "Because I needed you."

His words hit me right in the chest, and I stare at him, for so long my fingers begin to tremble around my bottle of vodka.

"That makes you so much darker than me," I whisper.

He opens his eyes and tips his head to the side. "Except you needed it as much as I did, so again, we're the same."

I hold his gaze, something inside me stirring.

A feeling I know I should fight.

Keep locked down.

But it's so damned hard when he's sitting there, looking at me the way he is right now, his eyes soft for the first time ever.

"Maybe we are," I murmur.

"Yeah." He closes his eyes again. "Maybe."

With that, he's asleep.

With that, I'm even more confused than ever.

# 8

*"Please, Mommy, don't hurt me," I cry, struggling to keep my head above water.*

*"You're not safe anymore. If Mommy goes away, you won't be safe. We have to do this."*

*"Mommy, please," I cry.*

*"We will go together, just me and you, Willow. Forever."*

*Water swarms my mouth as she pushes my head under the water. My tiny feet kick, and I squirm desperately. I can't breathe; I'm not strong enough to escape her. I cry out for my daddy, but he doesn't hear me. I'm trapped and, soon, darkness takes over.*

I bolt upright screaming and gasping for air. I grip my throat, wheezing and choking. I can't breathe, I can't breathe. I roll off the couch and fall to my knees on the floor. I pound my fist into my chest, but I can't breathe. I can't breathe. Jagger is beside me in minutes. I didn't even realize I had fallen asleep on the couch with him.

"Willow," he barks, groggily. "What's wrong?"

"I can't breathe," I gasp, slamming my hands into my chest again, eyes clenched shut.

My body has forgotten how. It always forgets how when I have that dream.

Jagger grips my shoulders and hauls me up, bringing me close to his face.

"Look at me!" he orders.

I open my eyes, heaving and panting. I'm going to pass out. Soon, I'm going to hit the deck.

"Do what I'm doing," he growls, grip so tight it hurts, but he's keeping me from falling. "Breathe in through your mouth."

I shake my head. "I can't."

"You can!"

I struggle to take a deep breath and only a little bit gets in, and when it does it burns, as if I have been shoved into the water without air.

"Another, come on."

I try again, this time it gets a little further.

"Keep going."

We repeat this for a few minutes until I'm breathing properly again and my shaking has subsided. I close my eyes and wipe my hand over my face, trying to remove the sweat beading on my skin. My hands are still shaking as the dream lingers in my mind. Only, it's not a dream. It's reality. A situation that will forever haunt me. Jagger grips my chin and tilts my head back, forcing me to look at him.

"What just happened?"

"Nightmare, it's nothing," I mumble.

"That was no nightmare. Tell me what happened."

With trembling fingers, I jerk out of his grips. Oh, he wants to talk to me now? He's the one who triggered all of these memories. He's the one who ripped me from my life, and now he wants to talk, to be the hero? My entire body is shaking as I look him in the eyes.

"My life is none of your business, Jagger. I never asked for any of this so stop pretending like you care about the memories that consume my fucking brain. You're the reason I'm here. You're the reason I'm losing it. This—" I shove a finger into my chest "—is your fault."

I spin on my heel and rush toward my room, slamming the door loudly when I get in. I drop to my knees and cry. My mind is consuming me, spinning around and around until I can't breathe. I heave and shake until there is nothing left in my body. It's only then I hear the sounds coming from outside, the slamming sounds, the glass breaking, things smashing. I wipe away my tears with the back of my hand and slowly stand.

When I get out into the living area, Jagger is standing by the window, his arms above his head and his forehead resting against the glass. His knuckles are bruised and battered and he's heaving. There are lamps strewn about, broken glasses, and the dining table is overturned and on the ground, one of the legs broken.

Something about the way he looks right now touches a piece of my heart I wasn't sure he'd ever get to.

I stare at him for the longest moment, unsure if I should go over or not. I want to, everything inside me screams to comfort him, but I still doubt myself. This situation, it's toxic, and yet I can't seem to help myself. Jagger makes me feel things I've never felt before, and those things terrify me. They're not healthy, I know they're not healthy, but I still find myself stepping forward, and, when I reach him, I place my hands on his back. He tenses but doesn't turn.

I run my fingertips up and down, slowly, feeling him shiver lightly beneath my touch. I trace little circles and then move my hands lower and over his perfect, firm backside. He sucks in a breath but still doesn't turn. I press myself closer to him, crushing my breasts against his back and reaching around to cup his abdomen. My fingers slip beneath his shirt and stroke over his muscles.

I'm playing with fire.

The most fucked up inferno I could ever have imagined.

I press my lips to the skin near the back of his neck, and he tenses. I slide my hands up beneath his shirt, and over his smooth, perfect skin.

I close my eyes, taking in the moment, not believing he's actually letting me touch him, and mostly, not believing how much I'm liking it. This is fucked up. I'm fucked up. He's fucked up. He stiffens and reaches up, closing his hands over mine through his shirt, stopping me. His breathing becomes ragged and, finally, he turns.

My hands are forced to slip from his skin.

"Willow …"

"We're so fucked up, you and I. Aren't we?" I murmur, stepping so close my body is pressed against his once more.

His hands go to my hips, but he doesn't push me away. "This is wrong. I kidnapped you. You're my captive. What you feel … it isn't real."

"The funny thing about that is," I laugh, bitterly. "I don't fucking care anymore."

I stare into those beautiful blue eyes and I'm lost. My feelings for this man are no doubt a result of the fact that he's been all I've had for the last few months, and I know they're likely not real, but I feel them all the same. He strokes my cheek, and, in the background, music is playing. I didn't notice until now, it's so faint. Jagger pushes me out into the middle of the living room and wraps his arms around me. Before I know it, we're dancing.

I don't dare speak, afraid to ruin this moment between us. Our bodies are moving together and our eyes are locked. It's the moment where everything comes together and begins to make sense. I know as crazy as it is, my life will never be the same again. Not now. Not after this. The thought both scares and excites me at the same time. I swallow when Jagger moves his head down, capturing my lips in a gentle caress.

I whimper as sparks of life come into my body, the same way they did the last time he put his mouth on me. My lips mold with his and he's moving them over mine gently, softly, bringing me to heights I never thought I could find. He pulls me closer, and I tangle my fingers into the curl of hair at the base of his neck.

"I need you," I say, looking up at him. "I don't care if it's wrong. I need you."

He stares at me, his eyes second guessing everything for a single moment, then, I'm being scooped into his arms and he strides with purpose to his room. When he flicks the light on, I look around. I've never been into Jagger's room, but it's very nice. He has a big four-post king-sized bed in the middle of the room with dark maroon coverings. He has a big, black Persian rug on the floor and some very exquisite paintings on the walls.

He walks over to the bed and lays me down gently, careful not to hurt me in any way. I don't break contact with his eyes as he slowly removes my shirt and bra. His gaze, hungry and desperate, slides over my naked breasts. He kneels and takes hold of my pants, sliding them down my legs, taking my panties with them. When he tosses them aside, he begins kissing up my calves and thighs, fingers gripping my legs as he moves. I fall back, desperate for more.

When he reaches my pussy, he takes my knees and pushes them gently apart so he can expose me to his hungry gaze. He strokes gently, sliding his finger over my clit and down over my damp entrance. Then he brings his finger to his lips and sucks it, never taking his eyes off mine. I groan and arch, that sight is so erotic. He leans down, and I hold my breath in anticipation as he slides his tongue from my entrance right up to my aching clit. I cry out and tangle my fingers through the bed sheets.

This. This is what I've been waiting for.

"Oh god," I gasp.

He sucks my clit into his mouth, drawing an intense shudder from my body. I writhe, so needy, so desperate for more.

He slides one finger inside me and sucks my clit furiously until I'm bucking and screaming with a powerful release.

Only then does he release me, kissing the insides of my thighs before moving up my body, pausing at the scar on my stomach, but he doesn't ask about it. He kisses little circles all over it and then continues moving up until he reaches my nipples. He sucks each little bud until they form hard peaks, then he moves to my mouth. I can taste myself on him when he slides his tongue in to gently tease mine.

"I need you," I breathe. "Right now."

"Greedy, aren't you?"

"Yes," I whimper.

He grips his jeans and yanks them down, shuffling until he can kick them off. Then he positions himself over me, propping himself up on his elbows, his eyes locking with mine, his body hard. He feels so good against me. I can feel his aching cock against my entrance. He won't push it in, and I thrust my hips up, begging for him to fuck me. He smiles down at me, and the sight is truly breathtaking.

Out of this world spectacular.

The best thing I've ever seen.

"You look beautiful when you smile," I whisper.

He stops smiling and his gaze becomes intense again, like the words tear at something inside him that he wishes to keep hidden.

He grips my thighs and forces my legs around him. Then he thrusts inside me so quickly and painfully I cry out, my teeth finding the flesh on his shoulder where I clamp down, giving him a taste of his own medicine.

"Ouch, fuck," he growls.

"You're hurting me!" I growl.

He stops, exhales, then puts his head into the crook of my neck and sighs.

"If you don't want this," I whisper. "Then just stop."

"I want it."

"Then why did you hurt me?"

He doesn't answer, he just thrusts his hips, gentler this time, and sends a shiver through me. I cling to him as he pulls back and does it again. His hard length slides in and out, caressing that spot until I'm building higher and higher, desperate for release. He doesn't move his head from my shoulder, he just thrusts and thrusts with such desperation it hurts my heart. He's detached. One comment and he's detached. Gone. No longer with me in the way he was before.

He's fucking me. Finding release.

That's it.

"Jagger," I plead. "If you don't …"

He thrusts harder, slamming into me with such force it hurts. I cry out and shove at his chest, but he doesn't stop.

"Stop," I yell, shocking even myself, as hot tears burn under my eyelids.

He comes to an abrupt halt and slumps down on top of me, not moving his face from my shoulder, his breathing ragged. We both lie there for a moment, still, nothing but our breathing filling the quiet space. He finally lifts his head, and his eyes are wild and confused.

"What the hell is wrong with you?" I whisper, shaking my head.

"I'm fucked up, that's what's wrong with me," he growls. "We can't do this."

He moves to pull out of me, but the friction turns my sob into a guttural moan. He stills, no doubt confused, his eyes lock onto mine with question. Should he go on? I don't want him out of me. I want him right here. I want him to stay. I push my hips up, giving him the invitation he is seeking, and he slides back in and begins fucking me once more, slower this time. His pace is soft and gentle, bringing me to the edge. He gently rocks his hips, letting off little growls of pleasure while he drives me to the edge.

"Oh … God …" I scream as I shudder around him with my first orgasm.

He grunts, and then I feel him pulsing inside me. His release is silent, aside from that one, pained grunt.

When he stops moving, we both lie there, neither of us speaking.

I know what he's thinking—this situation is fucked up. It's wrong in so many ways, hell, that sex was wrong. So why do I want it to go on? He rolls away from me, falling onto his back and staring up at the ceiling.

"I should go," I dare to say, mostly because I have no idea what he wants in this moment.

"No."

It comes out hard and gritty, which tells me he means it.

"What's going on here?"

He doesn't answer.

"Jagger …"

"Nothing," he snaps, "nothing is goin' on here."

I sit up quickly. "We're doing that again, are we? You need to get your shit together, seriously."

I roll to get off the bed to leave, but he grips me and jerks me back down, rolling until he can flatten me with his body. He crushes my chest down onto the bed and his body lies over mine. He keeps me there, warm breath in my ear, dick hard against my bottom even though we only just finished having sex.

"You know the moment in life when everything you thought you were, is suddenly wrong? The moment that changes everything. It changes who you are, who you believe you are, and who you're going to be. You're that moment, Willow."

He whispers these words into my ear and my whole body gives way. I melt into the mattress, and into him. He doesn't move his body off mine, instead, he pushes into me once more, his cock sliding into my wet heat and causing a whimper to escape. He moves slowly over me, sliding his hips backward and forward until I am shuddering and crying out once more.

"I hate that I want you, but I can't stop," he whispers into my ear. "I can't stop this."

"I know," I gasp. "I know."

"Move your ass up, Willow. Let me fuck you deeper."

His words cause a shiver to run through me. I raise my ass and he takes my hips, driving harder into me. I groan and tangle my fingers in the sheets until I'm coming around him again. He brings me to orgasm with his fingers on my clit and his length sliding in and out of me at least two more times before he finally finds another release of his own.

When he rolls off me for the second time, I remain with my face down, my body weak and satisfied. I don't roll, I just lie on my stomach until he crawls up beside me. He wraps an arm around me and pulls me to his side. I don't say anything, I just lie there wondering what the hell we are doing. The feeling is real, and it isn't just one sided. He feels it too, his words prove that.

"Dark and twisted," he murmurs.

I roll to my back and stare up at the roof. He pushes up onto his elbow, fingers tracing over the scar on my belly once more.

"What happened?"

I sigh. "It's a long story."

"I've got all night."

"It's a side to me I'm not proud of."

"It's me you're talking to," he murmurs, finger still tracing over the jagged edge of the scar.

I close my eyes and sigh. "I did it to myself."

He sucks in a breath but doesn't say anything more. He lets me go on.

"I blamed myself for my mother's depression. I blamed myself for my family falling apart. I was an unhappy teen, my life was in turmoil. My mother, she's sick, really sick and we've been through a lot when it comes to her. I just ... felt like I had no way out."

He leans down, pressing his lips to the scar.

"I couldn't take the agony anymore. It was all just too much. One afternoon ... I smashed the window in the bathroom, and I sliced my stomach up so badly I nearly died. It was only that my sister came over and found me, by complete accident, otherwise I would be dead."

"Willow ..."

"I'm a broken candle, Jagger. You can't reignite a flame that's no longer there."

"Everything can be fixed. Everything. Tell me about your nightmares."

I shudder, wishing he didn't bring that up. "When I was four, my mother tried to kill me."

Best to just rip the bandaid off.

He sucks in a breath and his body stills. "What?"

"She thought it was for the best. She was sick, and she thought people would hurt me when she wasn't around. So, she thought she would do whatever she could to prevent that from happening. She's very unwell."

"I'm sorry that happened to you."

And yet, here I am, in another situation I can't control.

Only this one ... It doesn't feel so bad.

~*~*~*~

"Are you hungry?" Jagger asks, after a few hours of us just lying there, being one hundred percent ourselves.

Something that hasn't happened before.

My stomach growls in answer, and he snorts. He gets up and pulls on his jeans. I stare with pure female appreciation at the ass that fills out those jeans and the body that ripples when he moves. Jagger is so fucking gorgeous, and the worst part is, he knows it. When he walks out, I lie for a moment more before getting up and dressing myself. When I walk into the kitchen, he's digging through the cupboards.

"What do you want?"

I raise my brows. "You can cook?"

He grunts and turns to give me a look. "No."

"How did you survive before you kidnapped me and forced me to feed you?" I say, playfully.

"Frozen meals."

I scrunch up my nose. "That's bad for you."

"Then get over here and cook me something."

"No."

His eyes flash and he walks over to me, putting his hands on my hips and pressing me back into the bench. His lips come down close to mine, and I shiver.

"Are you defying me?"

"I might be."

"Hmmmmm …."

His lips graze my neck, and I shudder. I grip his sides, pressing my palms flat against his skin. It's hot beneath my hands and increases my want. I slide my hands up and around until I find his pecs. I knead them and he groans, nipping my earlobe.

"I can't go again, you're gonna kill me."

"Old man." I grin.

He huffs and pulls back, and I smile up at him innocently.

"Don't smile at me like that."

"I'll stop smiling at you when you feed me."

He turns with a snort and pulls out some bread, ham, and cheese. He whips together some sandwiches and hands me one. I'm so hungry this is gourmet. I bring it to my mouth and take a bite, moaning as my stomach rumbles with appreciation.

"Mmmmm, the simple ham sandwich." I grin. "It's the best I've got."

We eat in silence and talk for a few more hours about our lives and then finally head to bed. I go back to my own room, but I'm okay with it. I'm exhausted and feel like things have finally taken a turn. Will Jagger let me leave now? What does all of this mean for us? I know what we're doing is twisted and immoral, and it's probably far from being real, but tonight, it felt real. Our conversation felt real.

I fall into the first deep sleep I've had since I've been here.

I wake late in the morning, because I roll and feel something sticky between my legs. Opening my eyes, I groan and then reach down, pressing my hands to the wet spot and bringing them up to my face. Blood. Oh sweet Jesus. I never know when I'm going to get a period, and when I do they come on without warning and are very intense. How did I not feel that my period was coming? I haven't had one since I've been here — I should have guessed that it wasn't far off.

I stand and quickly make my way to the bathroom. I strip off my clothes and get into the shower, washing away the blood. It's then I realize I don't have any protection and I'm going to have to go out there, wash my bloodied sheets and ask my captor for god damned tampons. Like this could get any worse!

I finish up in the shower and use some toilet tissue to protect myself until I can ask Jagger for help. I go back into the room once I'm dressed and pull the sheets off the bed, bundling them up, and walk tentatively out into the kitchen. Jagger is standing in a pair of boxers, leaning over the counter looking at his phone. His eyes move up to stare at me when I appear.

"What're you doin' with all your sheets?"

"Ah," I don't know how to tell him this. God dammit, it's nothing to be ashamed of. "I got my period."

His eyes widen, but he gathers himself quickly. "I didn't think of that. Fuck. Sorry. I'll organize for you to get some protection."

God. I could curl up and die right now.

"That would be great. I'll put these in the wash and then, ah, tell you what I need."

I rush past him and put the sheets in to wash, then I meet him back in the kitchen. He's gathering up his keys, and I dare to ask the question I know he'll shoot me down for, but I can't help but try.

"Take me with you."

He exhales. "Can't do that, you know I can't do that. People are watching and looking for you. I can't risk it."

It was worth a shot.

I nod.

"What do you need?" he asks, looking uncomfortable again.

I clench my jaw for a moment. "Tampons. Just tampons."

"Right. Ah … what size?"

I lose it, a snort bubbles from my chest followed by laughter.

"What?" he grunts.

"Nothing, it's nothing. Just regular, please. And pads. I need some pads."

He looks like he's about to lose his shit now, too. "Pads?"

"Yes, sanitary napkins, underwear pads, whatever. You know, you stick them on and they stop you messing things up."

"I got it," he mutters.

"Never bought this stuff before, have you?"

He shakes his head. "No, it's a first."

"Well, best of luck in there."

He hesitates, shoving his keys into his pocket. "Anything else?"

"Chocolate. Wheat bag. Soda. Painkillers. Oh, and those yummy cheese puff things."

He gives me a look.

I smile.

He's about to learn just what a woman needs when she's on her period.

He should have thought of that before capturing me.

Karma is a bitch.

# 9

When Jagger gets back, I've finished washing the sheets, drying them, and remaking the bed. I have also cleaned the room, the kitchen, and am just finishing up with the final load of clothes I washed. God damn man took forever, and I was beginning to think I was going to have to use toilet paper forever.

"I got hit on," he grunts, tossing the bag of items onto the kitchen counter, "a lot."

I raise my brows. "For buying tampons?"

"Apparently, it's horribly sweet, kind, and generous of a 'boyfriend' to buy his 'girlfriend' tampons."

I bite my lip, trying not to laugh.

He opens the bag while I'm still fighting back a laugh. He tosses me three packets of tampons, two packets of pads, and some sort of period underwear. Then he pulls out chocolate, ice cream, frozen pizza, and a few rented movies.

"What's all that?"

"The girls said you'd be crazy hormonal and would need lots of bad, bad food. They also said movies, so … I got you some."

"The cheese puffs?" I question.

He gives me a look.

"Pushing it?"

"Pushing it," he grunts.

I take the bag of items and give him a grateful smile—he returns it weakly. He's not himself this morning, and I wonder what's going on. I walk into the bedroom and clean myself up, relieved that is over. When I'm cleaned up, I come out, and he's on the phone. He has his back to me, head dropped lower, and he talks quickly and harshly.

"Yeah, bring him over."

He hangs up the phone and turns to me, jerking a little when he notices me.

I narrow my eyes. "Is everything okay?"

He nods sharply, but as he begins looking for something in the kitchen, I can't help but notice how he's slamming things and cursing every time he can't find whatever it is he's looking for. Whoever was on the phone, it has him in a really bad mood.

"Jagger?"

He doesn't answer; he just slams a tin down on the counter and swears once more.

"Jagger," I say again.

He spins around to glare at me. "What?"

"What's the problem?"

"They've got your father. He's coming here."

My heart comes to an abrupt halt, and I stare at him. My father. They have my father. I knew that was the plan, that all along it was how this was going to end, but now that it's happening I don't know how to feel. The thought of seeing a man I thought was dead just makes everything inside me go numb. Heart racing, I look to the man who captured me, confused.

"You found him?" I whisper.

"Angel found his location, and they got hold of him last night. They'll be here in half an hour."

My heart sinks. He didn't come out on his own? If they found him, it means he didn't willingly come out.

"How did you find him if he didn't come out on his own?"

"He made calls, he was concerned enough to do that. It was enough to track him."

I nod. "Are you going to hurt him?"

He looks at me, and the expression on his face tells me the answer before he does. "If he doesn't provide what we need, we can't just let him go."

I straighten my back, and, without another word, I turn and walk into my room. My emotions are shot and I'm confused. I'm so god damned confused. I don't know if I'm angry at my father, or Jagger, or both, or just myself for feeling anything at all. I never thought I'd see him again, but now the reality is that I might, and it might be the last time.

For real.

I don't even know how I feel about home anymore. I dread the idea that I might look over my shoulder for the rest of my life if this all goes wrong. I don't know what is happening between Jagger and me, but the reality is that now he has my father, he has no use for me. Does that mean he'll let me go? Does he want me to stay? Does he want me to go?

I don't know.

The not knowing confuses me.

I'm in the middle of pondering how the next stage of my life will go when I hear the voices outside. He's here, my dad, the man I thought was dead, is here. I take a deep breath and decide I want to see him, I want to confront him, I want to know why he decided to leave us in danger. Taking a deep, shaky breath, I step out the door and there he is, cuffed and sitting on the couch surrounded by the guys.

He turns his head slowly, his eyes fixating on me, and I feel a sob rise in my throat. I make a strangled sound and press a hand to my chest, the emotions swarming inside of me too much to handle. My father looks the same, with his reddish brown hair and light blue eyes. We share similar features, the same full lips and skin tone. His eyes stay on mine and what I'm seeing terrifies me. He looks dead, emotionless, broken.

"Dad?"

"They didn't hurt you, I'm glad."

His voice comes out monotone, void of any feeling.

That's it? After all these years, that's all I get.

"That's it?" I whisper. "You let me believe you're dead and that's all you can say?"

He looks away. "Sorry."

"Dad," I croak, a soul-crushing feeling consuming me. "It's me. It's Willow."

"I know who you are," he grinds out. "You shouldn't be here. I shouldn't be here."

"Dad ..."

"Can someone please get her out of here?"

"Jagger?" I say, looking to him.

Jagger's face is tight. "You heard him, Willow. You need to leave."

Pain, a pressure-filled pain, crushes my chest. I turn when Ace steps toward me, jerking my hand out to stop him. I don't need him to drag me out of here. I can take myself. I can take myself out of this god damned house and away from all of them. I spin around and rush away. When I get into my room, I begin grabbing the few things I have with me and shoving them into an old plastic bag. Jagger comes in behind me, and his eyes fall on my bags.

"What're you doing?"

"You have him," I mutter, trying to fight back the emotion threatening to consume me. "A promise is a promise, Jagger."

He stares at me, his blue eyes intense. "I guess it is."

"Well then, I'm free to go, right?"

He looks away, his face hardening. "Right."

"And the other gang, am I safe?"

"I have what they want, they have no reason to go anywhere near you now. They will come after me. I don't think you're in danger. Angel said they know we have your father."

"So, that's it?"

He shrugs, his face stony hard. "That's it. It's all over for you."

"And ... us?"

"You and I are both clear that there is no us."

His voice is hard, but something in his eyes ... No. I can't analyze this. He doesn't want me here—if he did, he would say it. He would. Wouldn't he?

"You're clear on that," I growl. "You didn't ask me."

"You just asked me to leave. You're packing up to fucking leave. If you have somethin' to say, Willow, say it now because I don't play fuckin' mind games."

Oh, he wants to be mad? I don't think so.

"What do you want, Jagger?" I snap, sick of the back and forth.

"Nothin', I want fuckin' nothin'. Just fuckin' leave."

He turns and walks out, and I stand, watching him go. I know I should speak up, but what can I possibly say?

I want to stay? No, I don't want to stay but I don't want to walk away from him either. I'm so fucking confused it hurts. For my own sanity, I have to leave and take the time to clear my head. I pick up my few things, and then I walk out of the room and down the stairs. I don't see my father again, they've taken him into the basement.

Taking a deep breath, I exit the house and walk to the truck that I know is Jagger's because I've seen him arrive in it before. I slide into the passenger seat, a heavy weight in my heart, the feeling that I'll never be okay again when I drive out of this house so intense I don't think I can handle it a second longer. Jagger appears a moment later, getting into the driver's seat.

He doesn't say a word.

He could, but he's choosing not to.

He's giving me the answers, I don't have to ask him for them.

We drive for a solid two hours before I finally see the city. Where the hell did he have me? My stomach twists at the idea of going home. I've wanted it for so long, so why does it hurt so much? When we pull up at my apartment complex, it doesn't surprise me that he knows where I live. He hands me my handbag and I gasp.

"You had this the whole time?"

"Of course I fuckin' did."

He pulls out my phone and thrusts it at me. "My number is in there, if anyone bothers you or anything happens, call me. You're not completely safe until I get rid of Manchez. You tell the police anything, I'll come for you."

His words are like a knife to the heart.

He is threatening me.

On our last encounter, he's threatening me.

"Are we clear?" he grinds out, glaring at me.

"Are you done?" I snap.

I pull the phone from his hand, and his fingers graze mine. I look up and meet his gaze. I wait — part of me hoping he will say something and break this awful silence — but he simply turns and stares out the front.

"Remember what I said."

"That's it?" I whisper.

"What more do you fuckin' want from me? You were my captive. Nothing more. A bargaining chip. I've got what I want. I'm holding up my end of the deal, now get the fuck out of my car."

I nod, swallowing, and step out of the car. He plants his foot down as soon as I've shut the door, and angry tears course down my face. It's over. It's all over. What will I do now? How can I possibly ever be normal again?

Why is my heart breaking so badly that I want to turn and beg him to take me back?

Why doesn't freedom feel good?

What is wrong with me?

~*~*~*~

I'll never forget Ava's face when she opens the door to see me standing pitifully on the doorstep. She screams, and then crumbles with me in her arms to the floor where we sob and cling to each other for so long my legs go numb. I know how worried she must have been, I know she probably blames herself. When we get inside, she shuts the door and helps me sit on the couch.

"I'm dreaming, I must be dreaming. This can't be real? You're here. How are you here?"

She strokes my face and sobs incoherently, until I soothe her by assuring her that I'm okay. How strange, I'm soothing *her*.

"What happened?" she finally manages, swiping away her tears.

Lying isn't in my nature, so I tell her everything, from start to finish. By the time I'm done, she's sobbing again and wrapping her arms around herself, as if that'll make the pain go away. It won't, I've tried it.

"You need to contact the police, we need to go in there right now."

"No," I say firmly, my voice unwavering. "If you call them, I will lie. I will deny it. I will do everything in my power to make sure they never find him. Don't call them Ava, promise me."

Her eyes widen. "He kidnapped you, you were abused, he needs to go to prison for a very fucking long time."

"It wasn't so bad," I say, exhausted, tired, my body just so damned numb. "For a while, it was, but in the end it was like I lived there. He let me go. He promised he would and he did."

"Oh, God," she whispers, shaking her head. "You care about him, don't you?"

I look away, feeling my bottom lip tremble. Hearing her say those words out loud makes everything inside me feel that much more real.

"Oh, Willow, it's not real. You know that, right? It's fake emotions because he was your light in a dark time. Honey, it's not real."

"I know what's real and what's not," I croak through my brewing tears. "He didn't hurt me."

"No, he just took you to a place and let everyone else hurt you."

I swallow the lump in my throat. "You don't understand, it could have been so much worse for me."

"How?" she snaps, and then closes her eyes to gather her composure.

"If the other gang had been the ones to take me, I wouldn't be sitting here right now. He let me go, Ava. He promised he would and he did."

"What about now? You could be in danger."

I cover my face and sigh. "Ava, the gang have no reason to come anywhere near me now. They want what Jagger has. They will go after him to get it, not me."

"Willow …"

"If anyone is to blame here, it's my father," I spew out, waving my hands, frustration bubbling in my chest.

I don't want to explain myself.

I don't want to.

"I still think you need to go to the police—this situation is dangerous and you need their help."

"No," I say, sharply. "I said no."

"At least get some help, Willow, please."

I look away. "I'm fine."

She narrows her eyes. "No, you're not."

"I will be. I just need time."

"You're not going to stay in contact with him, are you?"

I think about Jagger's number in my phone and decide not to tell her about it. I don't even know if I can process the fact that I have it.

"I wouldn't know how to find him if I tried."

I just broke my no lying rule.

"We should call Jenny. She's been beside herself with worry. We thought you were dead."

Poor Jenny. It would have been so hard on her. "I will call her in the morning. Please, I just need tonight."

She hugs me again and strokes my hair. "Okay. I'm going to make you some tea."

I nod weakly and stand. "I'm going to shower."

"Take your time. I'll be right here."

I turn just as I reach the hall and call out her name. She turns and stares at me.

"It wasn't your fault, Ava, you know that, right?"

Her lip trembles. "I shouldn't have pushed you to go and approach him. I practically threw you at him. I should have watched you, I shouldn't have taken you in the first place …"

I walk over, placing my hands on her shoulders. "Ava, don't. I made my own choices that night."

I hug her again then disappear down the hallway. I head to my room. It has been so long, it all feels foreign to me, and I feel out of place. I stare around and look at the clothes on the floor. They are still there from the night we went out and I threw them all onto the ground trying to find the perfect outfit. If I had have stayed home that night … *No* … I can't think like that.

I reach into my purse and pull out my phone. When I switch it on, I can see right away it has been wiped clean and a new sim card has been installed. Jagger isn't stupid. Not even close. I open his number and stare at it for so long my vision blurs. I throw it onto the bed and, with a pain in my heart, get into the shower. I wash everything away, the last few months, all of it.

I pray it stays gone.

I don't know if I can take much more.

# 10

The next week of my life is a painful blur. I spend hours at the police department, lying through my teeth to protect a man who doesn't even want me. I tell them I was blindfolded and didn't see or hear anything the entire time I was there. I tell them I was in a room, held captive. I tell them a little, just enough to make my story believable. I tell them whoever took me was after my father, who is apparently in witness protection. They have a great deal of questions for me, but none of them can lead back to Jagger.

I just continue to lie. Over and over again.

I continued to beg Ava to agree with me, but my fear is that she'll break. I have to stick to my story, even if she tells another one. Without information, there is no way for them to know who took me. She isn't happy about it, she believes Jagger should go to prison for what he did, but I don't agree. I just want to get on with my life, and I hope one day soon, she can come to the same conclusion.

My sister Jenny cried for an entire day when she found out I was home. The press had a field day, but with no information, they could only make up stories. I was kidnapped and returned, and the reason behind it was still a mystery. I didn't tell Jenny the real story, and I made Ava promise not to tell her, either. She wouldn't understand. She'd never understand. Especially not when it comes to my father.

I assured Ava I would seek therapy, and I found a lady I could speak to without it getting out to the media. There is no way in hell I'm going to share the real truth with her, so I decide to give her a version of the truth. Everyone knows I got kidnapped, but as far as they know, I don't know who that person was.

I'm sitting in her office on day eight, staring at the wall with a grim expression. Doctor Peterson is a tall, pretty woman with flaming red hair and blue eyes. She smiles a lot and nods her head constantly, as though she's agreeing with everything I'm saying, which I know she's not.

"So, what happened after you two had sex?"

I glare at her. "Made love. We made love."

She nods again, fuck her damned head nodding. "I think you believe you made love, but making love is for people *in love*. From what you've told me, this man didn't love you."

"He took care of me. He didn't have to and he did. We connected. At the end, there was something there, something real …"

"Caring and loving are two different things, Willow."

"I know that," I snap.

"Why don't we look at the fact that he hasn't contacted you at all this past week? If he cares about you, why would he just leave and not come back for you?"

"I told him not to, and there is also the fact that he'd be arrested on the spot."

"You don't think a man in love would try anyway?"

I growl, frustrated.

"The feelings you're experiencing, they're not real, Willow."

"I know what you're thinking, and I don't have it. I don't have Stockholm's Syndrome."

She exhales. "I didn't say that. While it's common in kidnapping victims, I believe your case is a little different. Your kidnapper didn't take you to hurt you, in a sense, he took you to protect you."

"How do you suppose that?" I cross my arms, leaning back into the chair.

"From what you tell me, the other option would have been much worse."

I never thought of it like that.

"Why don't you tell me more about your feelings for this man? Help me understand."

"I'm not crazy."

"I never said you were."

"My feelings aren't fake. They're very real."

"What makes you believe that statement is the truth?"

"Seriously, can we just drop it? I survived, I made it through, and I'm free. End of story."

She writes something down. "Why did you just change the subject, Willow?"

"Because I don't know how to answer you without sounding insane!"

"Then tell me, what is it that makes you want to be with him so badly?"

I glare at her. "I didn't say I want to be with him."

She leans back in her chair and writes down some more notes. "So you don't miss him?"

"I don't know," I yell. "I don't know!"

She nods and then closes her notebook. "I think that's enough for today. I want you to go home and think about why you defend him, why you resent him, why you've got feelings for him, and bring me some notes for our next session."

I don't thank her or say anything else. I just stand and walk out.

I can't deal with this.

I can't deal with her.

I can't deal with life.

I want to go back.

I want him.

What the fuck is wrong with me?

~*~*~*~

"Willow, it's okay. I don't expect you to come," Jenny says, tipping some sugar into her coffee.

It has been another three days, and I don't feel any better. I can't get him out of my head, and the more people tell me it wasn't real, the more I believe it was. My shrink tries to make sense of it, of me, but she's getting nowhere. I'm all over the place. I hate him. I want him. I resent him. I can't get anything right in my head. I haven't turned my phone on again since the first night I got home, and I refuse to. If he wanted to find me, he would.

It's very clear he doesn't.

I think that hurts the most.

"I don't mind, Jenny. I have to get back to life sooner rather than later," I say, sipping my coffee. It's Jenny's birthday tonight and she's having a party at a local club. She's trying to tell me I don't have to go but I need to feel like I'm not drowning for just one moment.

One single moment.

"I don't think you're ready," Ava says, agreeing with Jenny.

"It's not up to you to decide if I'm ready or not," I mutter, putting my coffee cup down a little harder than I'd like. "I want to be normal. I just want my life back, and you two are smothering me."

"You got kidnapped," Ava says, her voice careful. "We thought you were dead. You need to understand why we're feeling the way we are."

"I know," I say, exhaling. "I understand, but if I don't get back to normal soon, I'm going to drown. Do you understand? I can't take it anymore. I need some fresh air."

I stand and shove my coffee cup away, then I leave the apartment. Walking without thought for as far as my legs want to carry me. I know they have my best interests at heart, but they have to understand how hard it is for me. I am finding it hard to settle back in, Jagger is on my mind day and night, and I can't breathe right without him. That scares the hell out of me.

Once I've cleared my mind enough, I turn and head home. I am going to the party tonight, and I'm not going to spend a single second longer wallowing. As soon as I return, I shower, wash my hair, and get dressed. I pick a low-cut, black dress and leave my hair down, curling around my breasts. Jenny and Ava both look like they want to say something, but neither of them do. Instead, they get ready right along with me and we all leave together.

The club we've picked is quieter than most, hence why it was chosen. Jenny's friends find her and the squealing and happy birthdays begin.

It's a warm night out, but I have my hair down anyway because it covers my low cut, short dress. Why? Because my back is now permanently scarred from Snake's beating. I hate him for that, and I hope he rots in hell where he belongs.

The night starts off well — Ava and I groove on the dance floor, and I make sure all my drinks are purchased by me and only me. I get drunk very quickly, and for the first time in weeks, I feel good. I know it's not the right way to go about it, but to be free of those feelings for just a moment is a relief I didn't know I needed. Ava and I are shoving through the crowd for another drink when I see a group of men standing in the corner out of the way of the lights.

My heart feels like it comes to a skittering halt. Jagger and the boys are standing in the darkness, watching me. How long has he been here? Is he following me? Is he going to take me again? My eyes meet his, and I'm sure I see him flinch.

I grip Ava's hand. "We have to leave, now."

"Why, what's wrong?"

"He's here."

"What? Who?"

I nod my head and she turns, staring at Jagger. "Call the police."

"No, let's just go. Out back."

"Jenny?"

I scan the dance floor, but I can't see her. When I spot her at the bar, I push through the crowd before reaching her and taking her arm.

"We have to leave."

"What?" she asks, confused. "No way!"

"He's here."

That's enough for her. With wide eyes, she takes my hand and we rush out the back. We just get through the door when a hand grips my arm and spins me around. I scream and kick out, but Jagger's strong arms are around me, holding me tight. Jenny cries out and smacks him with her bag and Ava screams as Angel takes her and wraps his arms around her.

"I'm not gonna hurt her," Jagger growls as Ace reaches for Jenny, pulling her back.

"What do you want?" I cry, squirming.

Jagger pushes me against the wall, his hard body pressing into me and bringing me back to life. I'm drunk and it's impossible to try and push him away. His mouth goes down to my ear. I tremble when he whispers in it.

"We need to talk. It's urgent."

I nod, swallowing. Jagger lets me go and turns toward the girls who are both putting up one hell of a fight.

"I promise you she'll be safe."

"Let her go, you fucking asshole!" Ava cries, slapping Angel over and over again. "You touch her again I'll cut your dick off."

"Ava," I say, meeting her gaze. "I'll be okay. I promise."

"Willow, please," Jenny yells, trying to stomp on Ace's foot.

"I give you my word, I will drop her home as soon as I'm done," Jagger tells them.

Ava looks at me, her eyes wide and frightening. I give her a small smile and nod. She struggles as Angel and Ace drag her and Jenny to the car and shove them inside. Then they all get in and drive off.

"Where are they taking them?" I ask, heart racing.

"Home."

"Why are you here?" I ask, staring at the man who has been on my mind for the last week.

"We need to talk."

"I have nothing to say to you."

"You don't get a choice. Come on."

"Have you been following me?"

He stills and stares down at me. I get a good look at him under the streetlight. He's wearing a tight black tee and a dark jacket over top and oh, it looks gorgeous on him. His jeans are dark blue and he has a thick silver chain around his neck. His dark hair is messy, and he has a light shade of stubble on that beautiful jaw.

"Only tonight."

"Why?"

"Long story, get in."

He shoves me toward his truck, but I pause.

"I don't know if I can trust you."

"You don't get a choice," he growls.

I shake my head, crossing my arms over my chest, suddenly very cold.

His eyes go to my dress and his mouth tightens. "That dress is too fuckin' short."

"You don't get a choice in what I wear, Jagger."

"Get in the car, Willow."

"I don't …"

He reaches for me, taking my arm and swinging me around until my back slams against his truck and his hard body presses me against the cool metal. Then his lips are on mine and oh, I melt. I let my body fall against the car as he pushes his onto mine and secures me between the door and himself. I can't help my hands; they slide up his neck and tangle into his hair and I pull him deeper into the kiss.

He groans and runs his hands down the side of my body, making me shiver. "You're fuckin' toxic."

"You're the only toxic thing here," I pant.

He slides his hand up the inside of my thigh and finds my damp panties. I should be pushing him away, demanding he let me go, but here I am eating him up like he's my last meal. I can't get enough of him, I'm not sure I even have it in me to say no right now.

"So fuckin' wet for me," he growls.

"Yes," I moan when he slides his fingers under the fabric and finds my already aching clit.

I cling to him, needing him so badly I can't think straight. It's sick, twisted, and wrong, but for a moment, I feel like everything is right again. His free hand unbuckles his belt, and I feel him jerk his jeans down just enough to free his hard cock. In seconds, he has my leg around his hip and is thrusting inside me, deep and hard. I cry out and grip his arms, throwing my head back.

He thrusts with need, growling my name and crushing my lips. His arms are hard and tensing beneath my palms and his hips are thrashing, slamming my body against the car as he releases a world of frustration into me. His mouth moves down to bite my neck, and I cry out as an intense orgasm rips through my body. I shudder violently and tighten around him as he explodes with a hoarse growl.

When he stops thrusting, he pulls out of me and yanks his jeans back up. I pull my panties back into place and drop my leg, leaving my head leaning back on the car. I stare up at the stars, wondering what the hell just happened. Did we just fuck in a parking lot? Jagger takes my face and tilts it down to meet his. My head spins. I'm drunk. God, I'm drunk.

"I'm sorry to have to disrupt your life again."

That's all he has to say. Of course it is.

"Then why are you?" I whisper, hoarsely.

"It's important."

"Of course it is. So important that you could take the time to fuck me first."

He grumbles something and then opens the car door for me. I get in and wait for him to get around the other side. Surprisingly, he drives me to my apartment, and I see the other car out front. Relief floods me.

"Why are we here?"

"Because this involves all of you."

"What?"

"Just get inside."

Well, this has just gone from bad to worse.

# 11

I don't bother looking at Jagger as we walk inside the house.

My mind is a mess. I just slept with him. Just caved like a desperate woman in need. I should have held strong, but the moment I saw him everything disappeared and he was all I could see. I should know better by now.

We walk inside the house and the first thing I see is Ava standing by the kitchen counter, her arms crossed, glaring at Angel. The second she sees me, her face is full of relief as she rushes over, throwing her arms around me. I hug her tightly, thankful she's okay.

"Are you okay?"

"I'm fine, it's fine."

Jenny stays on the couch—she gives me a weak smile but she doesn't look so frightened anymore. Angel and Ace are here, the other men have gone. Angel nods his head at me, and I give him a brief nod in return. When Jagger walks in, Jenny stares at him with wide eyes; I know what she sees, he's beautiful. Ava already knows that, but it doesn't stop her from ogling him all the same.

"Why is he here?" Ava asks, leaning in close.

"Ask him," I mutter. "I don't know either."

Ava turns and glares at him, crossing her arms. "I don't know what you're doing here, or what you want, but you have some nerve coming in after what you did to Willow."

"Sit down," Jagger snaps, and Ava's eyes widen.

"You're not welcome here," she seethes.

God, this isn't getting us anywhere.

"Look, whatever he wants to say, I'm sure it's important or he wouldn't be here. Let's just find out what it is," I say, taking her hand and pulling her down onto the couch beside me.

Jagger looks around the apartment, eyes scanning over it, before turning to me. "Have you seen your father?"

I blink.

Jenny looks to me, confused. She doesn't know dad is alive, I didn't tell her that little piece of information.

"Way to go," I mutter.

"What?"

"She doesn't know," I exhale, turning toward Jenny. "Look, this isn't how I wanted to tell you any of this, but you need to know that my dad isn't dead, he's very much alive and that has a lot to do with why I was taken."

I take another deep breath, and I tell her everything. I hate the way her face scrunches, and she looks like she has been betrayed in the worst way. I know it hurts, I know it's shocking, I felt the same emotions when I found out. She sits in silence, processing the entire thing, and I take her hand into mine, squeezing it.

"To answer your question," I say to Jagger, "no, I haven't seen him."

"Well, he got away, and not only does he have us after him, but Manchez is after him, too. You're not safe. We're staying here until this is sorted. I'm afraid he will come for you to get your father out considering it worked so well for us."

"How the hell did he get away?" I ask, confused.

"Doesn't fuckin' matter," Ace grunts from the corner, telling me he had something to do with it but doesn't want to go into detail. "Fact is he's gone and you're all in danger."

"What?" Ava asks, narrowing her eyes. "It has nothing to do with us, why do we have to be involved?"

"Do you want Willow to stay here, or do you want me to take her again?" Jagger growls.

She glares at him. "She's not going anywhere with you, you're lucky you're not behind bars right now."

"Then," he grinds out, "we stay here. Where Willow is, danger is. End of story."

"What has he got that's so important?" Jenny finally asks, narrowing her eyes.

"That's none of your concern," Jagger tells her. "But he did mention something about Willow having the information before doing a runner."

"I have nothing of his." I shake my head, confused.

"He mentioned your mother, too, so I'm sure he might show there as well. Either way, whatever he hid, it has something to do with you and until we know where it is, we can't leave you unguarded."

"You expect me to believe my father left some sort of vital information near me?" I mutter, crossing my arms.

Jagger sighs. "Will you just fuckin' trust me, Willow?"

"Trust you?" Jenny cries laughing bitterly. "You stole her, and now you want us to trust you? I'm calling the police."

Jagger doesn't even flinch at her threat. "You call the police and you die, simple."

"You'll kill me?" she gasps.

"No, I wouldn't lay a hand on you. It's not me you should be worried about. You involve the police, you can kiss your life goodbye."

"You can't keep us prisoner," Ava yells, slamming her hand down on the coffee table.

"You're not fuckin' prisoner, I'm just going to be here until it's sorted. Then you can get back on your merry way and forget about me."

"How long until it's sorted?" I ask, the idea of having to be around Jagger again making everything inside me twist in confusion.

"Either your dad or Manchez will make a move. If it's Manchez we'll take him out and finish this. If it's your father, it's trickier because we have to draw Manchez out by using him."

"You're going to kill Manchez and his gang?" I gasp, eyes wide.

"That's the plan."

"We're going to live with a bunch of murderers?" Jenny says, looking to Ace and Angel, who are both standing, arms crossed, watching us.

"Call us what you want, I'm sure you'd rather this than be dead, wouldn't you?" Ace asks her, his voice gruff.

She flushes and looks down at her hands.

Jagger glances at me. "I know you didn't want to see me again, but I don't have much choice. Believe it or not, I'm protecting you."

"If you didn't bring me into this mess in the first place, you wouldn't have to protect me," I mutter.

"You would have been dragged into this mess regardless, once they found out your father was behind it, they were going to come after you. Be grateful I got you and not them."

"I've heard it all before," I huff. "Do we need to have escorts when we go out, or to work?"

"Yes, Angel will escort Ava, and Ace will escort Jenny if and when she's here."

I narrow my eyes. "Let me guess, I'm lucky enough to get you? He glares at me, and I sigh, spinning around. "We don't have much room."

"Ace and Angel can sleep in the living room. You can go in with Ava, I'll use your room."

"Why can't we go to your house?" I question.

"It's too risky. If they corner us there we have less chance of getting out. Here we're in a public place, less likely for an attack."

"Well, that's comforting, I'm sure I'll have nice dreams."

Jagger glares at me. "I can leave and let you deal with it all on your own, if that's what you'd prefer?"

I'm not arguing with him.

My brain is in too much of a scramble.

"Can I talk to the girls alone, please?"

"Fine. Angel, Ace, go get our shit from the truck."

I lead Jenny and Ava down the hall and into my room. I shut and lock the door and turn to them. The expression on their faces tells me they're less than pleased with this, but, if what Jagger is saying is true, they're in danger because of me and I can't let that happen. Perhaps I should just go back with Jagger?

Jenny doesn't live here, but she is always over visiting, and unless she's willing to spend no time with us, she's going to have to accept the situation, too.

"I'm so sorry," I tell them both. "If you like, I can suggest I go back with him."

Ava shoots me a look. "Absolutely not, you're staying right here where I can protect you. If they have to be in the house, too, so be it."

"I can't believe your father is alive," Jenny whispers, sitting on the end of the bed.

"I was shocked, too."

"And he's dealing with criminals, that makes it so much worse."

I nod. "I know."

We all sit on the bed, and I take their hands. "I know this situation is less than ideal, but until this is over, they're the best people to take care of us. We just have to trust what they say. I know that's hard, but they're not here to hurt us."

"Because they took such good care of you," Ava mutters.

"Ava, I know it looks bad, but we have to trust them. We're not safe anywhere else. Jenny, if you feel safer staying away until this is dealt with, that is your choice."

Jenny shakes her head. "I can deal with Backstreet Boy number one following me around, but there is no way I'm staying away from you. I thought you were dead. I'm not letting that happen again."

I laugh. "Backstreet Boy …"

She grins. "They're pretty hot, aren't they?"

"Hot assholes," I mutter.

"So, is Jagger his real name?" Ava asks, crossing her ankle over her knee.

"No, it's Johnny. Jagger is the club name so to speak—Johnny, Aiden, George, Greg, Eddie, and Rusty. They all go by nicknames, though, so you won't hear anyone call them by their real names."

"Oh …" Jenny says, nodding. "That's confusing."

"It is," I agree. "Just stick to Angel and Ace for now and you'll be fine."

"So that's it, we're now living with three hot, angry men?" Ava asks.

I nod, exhaling.

It's going to be an interesting few weeks.

~*~*~*~

"Seriously, Jagger, sleep on the floor," I growl, tossing a pillow and blanket onto the floor.

Jenny wanted to stay tonight, so she's sleeping with Ava, which left me no option but to sleep in my own bed with the man I'm trying so very hard to keep my distance from. He is refusing to leave my room, and considering there is no where else for him to sleep, I'm running out of options.

"I'm not sleeping on the fuckin' floor," he growls, taking his shirt off and tossing it on the ground.

I force myself to look away while muttering, "You wanted to come here."

"So?"

"So, you sleep on the floor."

"We fucked tonight, or did you just forget that?"

I smirk. "While that was a rather enjoyable experience, it still doesn't change my mind."

"Too bad."

He reaches down, picking up the pillow and blanket, then gets on the bed and slides in. I reach over and shove at his chest but he won't move.

"You're an asshole."

He shrugs, and I roll to my side, shoving a pillow between us. When the light is flicked off, I lie staring into the darkness for a long while. Just as I think he's asleep, he rolls and leans over me, whispering in my ear. "You don't really mind me being in your bed."

"I mind," I hiss.

"Bark at me all you want, act like you hate me, we both know you don't."

"I certainly don't like you," I point out.

"You wanted to come home. You chose that."

His words anger me, mostly because he's right, but also because I thought he might just stop me from doing so.

"You kidnapped me. You took me from my life. You confused my fucking brain. Then you just let me go. Don't come at me and twist things further."

"You could have spoken up," he growls.

"I'm going to sleep."

I roll over, and the room falls silent. It takes me hours to fall into a restless sleep, only to wake in the middle of a nightmare about Manchez. The dream is so real, I wake up screaming and thrashing, trying to escape the clutches of a man I don't even know. It has become somewhat of a fear lately, a fear of someone I've never even seen. Jagger has told me over and over how dangerous he is.

"Hey …"

A hard body is suddenly pressed against mine, big arms going around me until my face is crushed into a chest I've tried so very hard to forget.

"It was just a dream," he murmurs, groggily.

I reach for him, desperation taking over. I need comfort, I *want* comfort. I know how fucked up my mind is, but this man is consuming me, and I don't want to fight it any longer. I find his lips and desperately pull him to me. With a groan he slides his tongue into my mouth to dance with mine. We kiss until I'm panting and his body is heating against my own, his flesh alight with our desire. I move quickly, until I'm straddling his hips. His hard erection presses into my core, causing me to shiver.

I grip his face, deepening the kiss. My mind is hazy and I just want comfort. It's all I need. Just comfort. He's my comfort. He grips my panties and tears them off in one quick movement. No time for foreplay, just like earlier. We just want each other; I want him inside me, thrusting until it hurts. He grips his boxer shorts and pulls them down, and slowly lowers my pussy over his cock.

"God," I whimper, clinging to him as he sinks into me, stretching me wide.

I feel his piercings touching that sensitive spot inside me, and I cry out, rocking my hips and clawing at his chest.

He groans and grips my ass, using it to guide me up and down. I slide easily along his length, so aroused it hurts.

His ragged groans fill me and spur me on. I need all of him. Every bit I can get. He thrusts his hips upward, causing violent tremors to course through my body. When I cum around him, his growls fill my ears.

"Fuck!"

He pulses deep inside me, and I whimper when he clings to me and thrusts his hips upward to milk every last droplet out. When I come down from my high, I fall down onto his chest, face buried in the warmth there. We both fall silent, our panting the only sound that can be heard. I need to stop this. I know I do. But I can't. I'm so confused, so obsessed with this man, I don't know how to escape.

"Why do I keep doing this?" I whisper against his skin.

"We both know why," he murmurs.

"No, Jagger, I don't. It's toxic, it's dangerous, yet I keep coming back."

"Who said it was dangerous, toxic? Who?" he growls.

"You took me from my life. I went through hell because of you, and yet I'm so madly in …"

"In what?"

I shove away from him, sliding off until I fall onto my back on the bed. "It doesn't matter, it's wrong. Whatever I'm feeling, it isn't real. None of this is real. It's all a crazy headfuck, and it's going to cause more pain than I can handle."

"It is real. Whatever it was that we felt then wasn't created in your mind. Why don't you fuckin' trust your own judgment?"

"I have a weakness. My mother is in an institution because she has the same weakness. I don't trust it to lead me down the right path. This, it isn't normal. It's not okay. It's an obsession because of the way I am."

"You think you're weak? You've dealt with things others would never have been able to handle. You made it through, and you're still alive. What you feel is real, and just because your mother has a problem, doesn't mean you do, too. You're nothing like your mother …"

"You don't know that," I grind out, frustrated.

This conversation, it always triggers something in me I so desperately try to hide.

"Yes, I do."

"No, you don't …"

"Yes, I fuckin' do!" he barks.

I sit up, I can't take this any longer. "I have to go."

"Do not fuckin' leave this room."

"Please, don't do that again … you can't have sex with me. We can't … this is nothing, Jagger. It'll never be anything."

"You started that, not me," he points out, his voice tight.

"Well, I'm finishing it," I whisper, then turn and leave the room.

When I get to Jenny and Ava's bed, I crawl in and crumble. They don't say a word, they just pull me close and hold onto me until all my tears subside.

They know … *they know.*

Jagger is wrong.

I'm just like her.

# 12

The morning comes like a horrible cold. I know what I must face today, and I don't know how I'll do it. My home, my life, and my friend's lives have been invaded. I know it's for our own safety, but I can't get over the fact that our lives have just been put in danger, and we did nothing at all to deserve it. I hate my father for that right now.

I get up and slide out of the bed. Jenny is still curled up beside me, sleeping soundly. I walk out into the kitchen and Ava's standing with a coffee in hand, staring at the two half naked men sleeping on the couch, the expression on her face quite hilarious. I glance over at them and can't help but smile. Big bad boys in the daylight, but here and now, they just look like two normal men sleeping without a care in the world.

"I can't complain about the view and all, but seriously, I can't believe we have to be followed around for god knows how long," Ava mutters.

I laugh softly and pour a coffee. "I know, it's frustrating, but the alternative isn't something you want."

She nods. "I ran into Angel last night in the hall way, seriously, just slammed right into him. The man was half naked. Scared the life out of me."

I grin. "Well, it could be worse. He could be fat and hairy."

She nods in agreement. "Well, at least I get some nice eye candy while being trapped in my own home."

"I'm sorry again. I know this isn't the best situation to be in."

She steps forward, taking my hand and squeezing. "Like I said last night, you didn't get a choice. These men were coming after you either way. I'm kind of glad it was Jagger's boys and not the other ones. From what you have said anyway …"

I purse my lips in a frown. "By the sounds of it, we never want to meet Manchez and anyone in his gang."

"Well, I guess we should be grateful then. Have you seen Captain Cranky this morning, or are you two still fighting?"

I laugh at her choice of words. "No."

"Nice of him to enjoy your bed." She raises her brows, giving me a pointed look.

"Yeah, well, I did leave him there."

"Are you ready to tell me why?"

"Jagger and I aren't meant to be, Ava. It's dangerous, and it isn't real, it's making me crazy."

"What makes you think that?"

"I'm worried my feelings are toxic and created from a situation that was no good for me, or him, or anyone else. No way a genuine feeling can come from that."

"You think you have that Stockholm thing your therapist mentioned?"

"I think so."

"Well, it could be that, but I will admit, as much as it kills me to, he does look at you in this way …"

"Way?" I ask.

"Yeah, like you do something to him. Stir something deep inside his soul. It's quite intense."

"That doesn't mean it's real," I say, even though her words stir something inside me.

"It doesn't mean it isn't, either."

I give her a narrow-eyed look. "I thought you hated Jagger?"

"Oh, I do. Trust me. But you're my best friend, and I'm always going to be honest with you. Even if I don't like what I have to say."

I give her a truly grateful smile.

"Anyway, enough encouraging for the day. Go and kick that fine ass out of your bed and let's get some ground rules laid down."

"Rules?"

She grins. "Rules."

With a laugh, I saunter off down the hall. When I get into my room, Jagger is just stepping out of the shower, butt naked. I gasp and cover my eyes, an automatic reaction and one made with little thought. I feel stupid the second I do it, because it only makes me feel that much more child-like inside.

"Did you seriously just cover your eyes? Fuck, Willow, are we really goin' to behave like this?"

"No," I say, slamming my hands to my sides, trying not to stare at his perfect naked body.

God damn.

I hate how much I want him.

I glance at his face and see he's angry, his mouth a tight line, his eyes heavy and narrowed.

"I'm goin' out," he snaps, pulling on a pair of jeans and yanking on a black shirt.

Yep. Angry.

"Jagger ..."

He spins around and glares at me. "Do not fuck with me, Willow. You either want this or you don't, but don't you play with me the way you did last night. Do you fuckin' understand me? Get your shit together, and if you can't, stay the fuck away from me."

I stare wide-eyed and watch as he leaves the room, slamming the door so hard the wall shudders. God dammit. This is going from bad to worse.

I shower and get ready for the day, then head back out to the kitchen, but Jagger's gone. Angel is sitting on the couch staring at Jenny and Ava in the kitchen. Well, this is awkward.

"Is everything okay?" I ask, glancing at them all.

"Fine," Angel says, flashing me a grin.

I've never really seen Angel smile, or Ace for that matter. Both men keep to themselves most of the time, barely speaking unless Jagger specifically asks them to. I wonder what they're like, outside of all of this. What are their lives like? Do they have a family? Or is this all they are?

"Why do they have to stare at us?" Jenny whispers in my ear as she brushes past me.

I smile and huff lightly. "Well, you are gorgeous."

"Seriously, I'm going to go crazy by the end of this. If Ace keeps looking at me like I'm a piece of meat, I might punch him."

"Admit it," I say, pouring a coffee, "you love it."

She shoves me, but I catch her shy grin. Ava laughs and walks out of the kitchen with a book and a coffee. It's her morning tradition.

She sits outside on her old, ragged chair and reads with a coffee in hand. It's her quiet time.

I finish up my coffee and do some chores around the house, mostly to take my mind off wondering where Jagger went and feeling guilty that he's so angry at me.

The morning goes by quickly. Ace goes to the store and fills the fridges and pantry with food and drink. I chat with Angel about my father, and we all sit down to salad subs for lunch. I still haven't heard from Jagger by late afternoon, and I'm getting worried. What if something has happened to him? He was the one who told us all that it's dangerous out there, what if he got into trouble?

I ask Ace about it, but he brushes me off, telling me he's fine and not to worry.

When night falls, I hear a truck pull up. Moments later, Jagger literally staggers in the door, and flops down onto the couch. Jenny gives me a look, and I stand in the kitchen staring at him. Angel gives Jagger a long look, then glances at me before retreating to the back deck. I'm guessing he doesn't want to deal with this one. I'm not particularly sure I do, either.

"Where have you been?" I ask when he lifts the remote and starts flicking through the channels. I can smell the strong scent of whisky from here.

"What are you, my fuckin' mother?"

"Okay, you're still pissed," I mutter.

"Understatement."

I step closer, because I have a lot to say, when I get a waft of perfume. It's strong and obvious. Something inside me twists, a burst of jealousy I've never felt before in my life. My palms actually become sweaty and my internal reaction is going to be intense, if I don't get a grip on it, that is.

"Where did you go?" I ask, my voice tight.

"Strippers."

He says the word as if it's nothing more than a trip to the store. Anger bursts inside of me, anger I've fought for so damned long to keep locked away. I can't take it anymore, I can't take him, I can't take this situation, I can't take my own mind. I reach down and pick up the remote before throwing it, full throttle, at his head. It hits him hard, and a loud angry bellow leaves his lips as he spins on me.

"You're a god damned asshole," I bellow, throwing my hands up. "What sort of game are you playing?"

"Me?" he laughs, bitterly. "You're the one who can't get her shit together. Do you think I'm the kind of man to sit around while you go through your mental fuckin' crisis? I'm not. I'm so far from the man you want, it's best if you just get over it."

That hurts. God, that hurts so bad.

"That's low, even for you," I whisper, voice tight.

"Here's the thing, I don't fuckin' care."

He looks at me with those penetrating blue eyes, unwavering and fierce. Challenging me, daring me to fight him.

"I'm going out. I can't deal with this," I say, turning on my heel and going to the kitchen counter where my phone is.

"Bullshit you are," he barks.

I laugh, turning back toward him. "You can't fucking stop me."

"Watch me."

I reach the door, then lean down and scoop up his truck keys. Angel has reemerged followed by Ava, both of them with concerned expressions on their faces. I open the front door just as Jagger leaps to his feet. Luckily for me, he's drunk. I run as fast as my legs will carry me out to the truck. I manage to get inside and lock it just in time before Jagger reaches me, his big body wild with rage.

"Get out of the fuckin' truck," he yells, slapping the window with his hand.

"Eat a dick," I yell, trying to figure out this new, fancy key.

God dammit, why is it so hard to figure out?

"Open the damned door or I'll bust it open," he barks, pounding his fist on the glass as he moves around to the front of the truck, standing in the headlights, giving me a look that promises revenge if I so much as consider driving out of here.

"Move," I yell, "or I'll run you the fuck over."

I finally get the key in the ignition, and the truck roars to life. Jagger bellows something at me, but I throw it into reverse and hit my foot down on the accelerator, the truck flying with speed right out of the driveway. I don't look back as I pull onto the road and speed off, having absolutely no idea where I'm going, but knowing one thing for certain.

I can't do this with him anymore.

I have to cut ties.

Permanently.

~*~*~*~

I drive until my mind stops turning with the million thoughts threatening to take over. I finally reach a local bar and decide I'll get out, have a few drinks and cool off. My phone is blowing up, but I've turned it off for the moment, and now I'm going to unwind. I see Jagger in my mind as I switch off the truck and walk inside. I see his angry face, the way he reacted when I drove away. So casually he walked into my house, and how quickly that changed when I called his bluff.

"What can I get you?"

I look up at the bartender as soon as I reach the counter and see him smiling at me. It's a quiet night in here, and he's clearly looking for customers. It takes me a minute to answer him, and when I do, I simply say, "Whisky. Neat."

"Got you," he nods, grabbing a glass and filling it for me.

He slides it over the bar, and I hand him some cash before scooting onto a stool and bringing the burning liquid to my lips. God damn Jagger and his moods, his twisted games. He accuses me of playing, but he's the damned dealer in this game of poker. He's back and forth, hot and cold, and I'm done trying to figure him out. We're either something, or we're nothing. We can't be both.

"Penny for your thoughts?"

I look up from my glass to see a tall, handsome man sitting on the stool beside me. He has the darkest eyes I've ever seen, quite possibly black, and his hair is cut short. He's wearing a crisp black suit and has a smile on his face that makes me a little uneasy, but I choose to ignore that feeling, because I'm very highly strung right now.

"Am I that obvious?" I say, taking a sip.

He nods. "Indeed, you are. Let me guess, man troubles?"

I playfully roll my eyes. "Something like that."

"Well, I'll give you some advice. They're not worth your time."

"Coming from a man, that's some solid advice," I laugh, taking another sip of my drink.

It's strong, and I can feel the effects almost immediately.

"It's because I'm a man that I can tell you to stay away. We're no good."

"Oh, I know."

"You're a beautiful girl, don't hang your coat up on one mans door. Go and enjoy all of them."

I give him a look. "You're hitting on me, and I don't even know your name."

He grins, low and almost cold. "Perhaps I'm going to make you work for it."

I roll my eyes. "Of course you are. I don't work for any man, sorry."

He chuckles and takes another sip of his drink, finishing it before waving down the bartender and ordering two more. He slides the alcohol across to me and I take the glass, not passing up a free drink. I'm not exactly rolling in cash, considering I don't have a job right now.

"Thanks," I murmur.

"What's your name, or is that too much for me to ask?"

"Sherilyn," I answer, quickly and effortlessly.

I've learned never to give out my name to any stranger.

Not after him.

The look the stranger gives me, has my skin prickling again.

It's as if he knows I'm lying.

"And how do you spell that?"

Uneasy, I change the subject. "What brings you here, anyway?"

"I'm waiting for someone."

"A girlfriend, perhaps?"

He grins leaning in closer to me. "Perhaps."

Something about him is setting off all the alarm bells in my body. I should finish up this drink and leave, coming here was a very bad idea.

"Well," I say, shooting down the whisky, causing a burn the entire way down. "I should get going."

"You're not leaving yet, are you? We're only just getting started."

His eyes scan over me, and I know, in this moment, I have to get the hell out of here. Something about him is screaming at me that I'm not safe. I trust my gut, now more than ever.

"I have to leave," I mutter, scooting my chair back.

"Come now, Willow, we're not done."

I spin, staring at him. "How do you know my name?"

"He knows," A growl comes from behind me, "because he's been looking for you."

Jagger appears in the corner of my eye, his focus on the man sitting beside me. The man turns towards him, a grin on his face. "Wonderful to see you, Johnny. It has been a long time."

I dare to glance at Jagger, but he's not looking at me. "We're goin' to leave now, unless you want this to erupt right here," Jagger warns.

The man grins. "I was just having a drink, surely you're not so overprotective of your little captive here that you won't let her have some fun."

Who is this man?

"Get up," Jagger growls, reaching for my arm and curling his fingers around it before hauling me up.

The man grins. "I'll see you soon, Willow."

Jagger pulls me from the bar with such force I can barely keep up with him as he charges outside towards his truck. I see Bull parked behind his truck, with Angel in the front seat, both of them staring at me as Jagger stops at his truck, jerking the door open.

"What the hell is wrong with you?" I snap, pulling my arm from his.

"You have no fuckin' idea who that was, do you?"

I shake my head, confused.

"That was Manchez. You very nearly didn't see the light of another fuckin' day."

My blood runs cold and my stomach plummets. That was Manchez? I was right there with the enemy, and I didn't even know it. I swallow down the lump in my throat as Jagger shoves me into the truck. Then, he goes around the front, getting in and speeding off. Bull follows in his truck, and I sit in complete silence as Jagger calls him and gives him instructions to make sure we're not followed.

"I'm sorry," I say, my voice shaky.

Jagger finds a spot in the darkness, off the side of the highway down a dirt track and turns the truck off. He spins on me, eyes wild. "When I say I'm going to be staying with you to protect you, I'm not fucking joking. I'm not doing it for fun, Willow, I'm doing it to keep you alive. What the fuck were you thinking?"

Anger bubbles in my chest.

I fucked up, sure. But it's only because he drove me to it.

"You're joking, right?" I snap back. "You are the one that came into my house, drunk, which by the way you still are, and decided to tell me you were at a god damned strip club. I'm a woman, a woman with feelings, and you decided to stomp all over those because you can't handle what's going on here."

"What's going on here?" he laughs, bitterly. "Do share."

I can't take a single second more of this.

I lose it.

I completely lose it.

"You know what, Johnny," I scream, reaching over the seat and slapping him right across the fact, "Fuck you. Fuck everything about you. You're an abusive prick and I'm done trying to figure out why the hell I have any sort of feeling towards you. You took me from my life and I'm still here letting you control everything I do. I'm so sick of your mental games. You say I'm playing? The only person who can't get their shit together in this situation is you. You're a fucking broken piece of glass and I'm about to stomp you down until you shatter into a million pieces because I'm sick to death of trying to figure out if I can glue them back together. You want to fuck with me, fine, go ahead. I'm not going to stop you anymore, but know this, if you so much as lay a fucking hand on me again, I'll shoot you right in your god damned head. Either man up and face your feelings or stay the hell away from me."

I finish up with a gasp of air, my hands trembling with rage. Outside, rain pours down on the windshield, but I don't take my eyes off his.

I expect a reaction, of course.

But the reaction I get isn't the one I was waiting for.

"Are you done?"

I nod, turning to face the front. "Yep."

"Good, now it's my turn. You're right, I am broken. So fuckin' broken some days I don't even know my own mind. It terrifies me that I don't know every single part of who I am, but it's how it is. You weren't meant to matter, fuck, not even a little bit. But you do. You do matter and I'm so fuckin' tired of tryin' to figure out why that is. You're a god damned pain in my ass, but those weeks without you were the hardest of my life. You want me to man up, Willow? I'll man up. I want you so fuckin' bad that most days I forget how to think. Is that man enough for you?"

I stare at him and then I lunge.

Without thought I toss off my seatbelt and throw myself over the chair and onto his lap. My mouth smashes down on his, every answer I've been holding in coming out during that kiss. He growls and wraps his arms around me, kissing me until we're both panting and desperate for more. He pulls back, eyes hungry, voice hoarse. "Much as I'd love to finish this, we have to get out of here. It's not safe."

"At home then," I murmur, grazing his lips with mine.

"At home."

I don't know what this means, but my god…I'm ready to find out.

# 13

We return home and after a few phone calls, Jagger tells me we're safe for now. Then, we retreat to the shower because my god, I can't wait a second longer to have him. The moment we're alone, naked, in the shower and the warm water is on us, I'm on my knees, cock in hand, ready to make him beg. I want to taste him. I want him in my mouth, hard and hot while he groans above me. His head falls back onto the tiled wall as I side my tongue around his throbbing cock. His groaning is erotic, and I love to tease him. He deserves it after tonight.

"Fuck baby, suck me."

I snake my tongue out and lick the glistening head of his cock, he growls and thrusts his hips forward, but I don't take him in my mouth.

"Fuck, don't play with me."

"Say please."

"No."

I lick him again, causing a ragged groan to escape his lips.

"Say please," I order, teasing him some more.

"No. Fuck…"

"Say it," I murmur, running my tongue up and down, "and I'll suck this beautiful cock."

"Fuck. Please. Suck me. Now."

With a grin, I take him into my mouth, and I suck. I torment him with my lips and my tongue until he's arching and thrusting his cock upwards. I take his balls into my hand, and I gently roll them around, which only adds to his desperate pleas. I stop and start, teasing and taunting until he's cursing and gripping my hair, thrusting his cock into my mouth.

"I'm going to cum, fuck," he barks, jerking my hair.

I feel pulsing, and then moments later I taste the salty liquid as he spurts hot and hard into my mouth. I groan and swallow, sucking until he has nothing left. When he pulls away, I peek up at him through my lashes. He keeps his hands in my hair and raises me gently, bringing my lips to his. I wrap my arms around his neck, but he dodges the kiss I go to give him, making a laugh escape my lips.

"Let's go to bed," he growls. "I'm not done with you."

We get out of the shower, drying off and I watch as he turns and leaves the bathroom. He still has a real swagger about him, and I know he will pass out quickly when we hit the sheets, but I let him think he's going to make me scream all night long. I pull on a long tee and some panties and we slide into bed together. He rolls me so his chest is pressed against my back and his arms are wrapped around me.

"You know what you did tonight was dangerous, don't you?" I say, curling my fingers through his.

"Saved your life, though," he murmurs against my hair.

"You could have had an accident. You're drunk…"

"You could be with Manchez right now."

He makes a valid point.

"Promise me you won't do it again?"

"Promise," he murmurs, voice sleepy.

"Johnny?" I ask into the darkness.

"Mmmmm."

"What is this?"

"Don't know, do you?"

"No, but I know I want it."

"Yeah, me too."

That…that right there, it's all I need to know.

I close my eyes and let myself drift off into the best sleep I've had in months.

Finally.

~*~*~*~

"Are you sure you know what you're doing?" Ava whispers to me as I pour a coffee the next morning.

"I have no idea," I say. "But…I can't keep fighting it. Whatever this is, I want it."

"I get that, I do. I just don't want you to get hurt…"

I face my best friend and put my hands on her shoulders. "I know and I love you for that, but I have to do what is right for me."

"And that's him?"

I nod. "That's him."

She smiles, hesitant, but she knows there isn't much she can do to change my mind about this.

"Just be careful, okay?"

"Always," I say, turning back to my coffee.

A few minutes later, Jenny walks into the kitchen, pouting.

"There's a fucking skid mark in the toilet."

Ava and I burst out laughing, causing Ace to bolt upright from his spot on the floor. Jenny frowns at us, but moments later she's laughing, too.

"I can't believe we have to live with three men," Ava chuckles.

"They aren't so bad…" I say, still grinning.

"Well, at least they're nice to look at," Jenny mutters, staring at the two men in the living area.

Angel stands, wearing only boxer shorts. When he smiles, he has a killer grin. He's gorgeous and he knows it. Ava flushes when he stares at her, and keeping the grin, he winks.

"Did he just wink at you?" I ask, eyes wide.

"I was walking to the bathroom last night and I slammed into him, again! This time though, he was naked and hard. I'm not joking, hard as a rock. I'm sure he's doing it on purpose," she whispers, watching him walk out of the room.

"You copped a feel of Angel's dick?" I ask, before bursting out laughing.

"Shut up! This is all your fault!"

Jagger walks in, his hair all ruffled, shirtless, looking so damned good we all stare as he as he runs his hands through his hair in an attempt to straighten it up.

"Take a picture ladies, it lasts longer," he mutters.

We all burst out laughing. He grins and walks over to me, wrapping his arms around my waist and pulling me in for a kiss so damned good I can't help the little moan that leaves my lips when he pulls away. Ava gives me a disgusted look, but her eyes are twinkling, and I'll take that as a good sign.

I'm distracted when my phone rings and I glance down to see the institution my mother is in calling. They never call. Hell, I haven't heard from them since before I got taken by Jagger. I look to Ava and her eyes go to the phone, then back up to mine. She looks worried. Jenny walks into the kitchen, looking between the two of us as I pick it up.

"Hello?" I answer.

"Willow, it's Sarah."

"Is everything ok?"

"It's your mother. She's lost it. Willow, she had a visitor yesterday and now she's beside herself. Something's really upset her, and she keeps asking for you. I don't know who the visitor was, the other ladies said it was a man and that she agreed to see him. I don't know what's happening."

My blood runs cold.

"Do you know his name?"

"Kane, I believe. Sorry, I don't know more. I wasn't here."

I swallow and shudder. My father visited her, just like Jagger predicted. I don't have a great deal of time for my mother but seeing someone she thought was dead isn't something anyone should have to endure. I know how that must have gone down in her mind and it wouldn't have been good.

"I'm coming. Give me two hours."

"Thank you."

She hangs up and I put my phone down, turning to glance at the girls.

"Mom?" Jenny asks.

I nod.

"What's wrong?" Jagger asks, returning to the kitchen and catching a look at my expression.

Do I tell him?

Mom won't talk to me if someone else is around, she's very strange with visitors. I need to know what my father wanted and the only way to do that is for me to go alone, but it's not safe for me to do so.

"I need to go and visit my mother, will you take me?" I ask.

He studies me, then nods. "Everything okay?"

"Yeah, they said she's been asking for me. If I don't go it'll cause her more upset."

Jagger nods again, but he doesn't look like he believes my story. Still, he doesn't argue. I get dressed and then we get into his truck and begin the journey to visit her. The drive is quiet, too quiet, and after a few moments it's clear that Jagger isn't falling for my lies.

"You sure everything is good?"

I'm staring out the window, so many things are going through my mind right now.

"Yeah, everything is fine."

"Everything don't seem fine. Don't lie to me, Willow…"

"I'm not lying to you," I snap. "I just don't like visiting my mother, okay? You good with that."

He exhales but doesn't push any further.

When we arrive, Jagger tells me he'll wait in the car to make sure I'm not followed in. I nod and get out without another word, walking inside.

I'm not ready for this.

I'm never ready for this.

## 14

"You look well, honey."

Sarah, the lady who has been working here for as long as I can remember, hugs me the moment I step through the front doors. She's lovely and has always been so kind to me the few times I've been in here. She knows what it's like and she understands. She's also really good to mom, which is something that isn't always easy to do.

"Thanks," I smile weakly, pulling back. "How is she?"

"Better knowing you are coming."

"I'm sure," I mutter. "Let's go then."

She signs me in and then walks me through security and down the peach-colored halls. The rooms are all secured with keypads on the doors, and in the more serious sections, guards. When we get to my mother's room, Sarah punches in the code and opens the door. It takes me a moment to be able to step inside, mostly because I'm terrified of how this will go, but after a deep breath, I manage to force myself.

My mother is sitting by the window, staring out. Her once radiant red hair is pulled back into a plait and is now dull. She has lost weight, I can tell that before she even turns to face us. The moment she does, her eyes fall on me and flare, just a touch. I give her a weak smile. She stands and walks over, taking my face in her hands. I close my eyes; I don't deal well with my mother touching me. She pulls me in for a hug like always, and I let her. I don't hug her back, just pat her weakly.

"Mom, is everything okay?" I ask, pulling myself away from her.

"Sarah, may I speak to her alone?"

My mothers voice comes out soft and whimsical. Very unlike the voice I remember.

"Yes, of course. I'll be right outside."

Sarah leaves and I sit down at the table in the center of the room. My mother joins me.

"Were you going to tell me?"

She gets right to the point, her voice no longer soft like it was a second ago.

"I haven't had the chance, mom. You know I have been through a lot."

She stares at me. "I thought he was dead. All these years he let me suffer."

Of course it's about her. It always is.

"It wasn't easy to take for any of us. Jenny is devastated, too."

"He's not even her father," she scoffs, shaking her head, "all this time he has been out there while I've been mourning."

God.

Here we go.

"Well, he's a liar. What can I say," I mutter, "I just wanted to see if you were okay."

She glances at the open door, then back to me and leans in closer. "He told me you were taken by some gang and were in danger. Is that true?"

I exhale. "He's the one who caused it all in the first place and the only reason I'm involved is because he got me involved."

"He gave me some things," she whispers, her eyes getting a touch wider, "and told me to give them to you."

I narrow my eyes. "What did he say?"

"He said I had to give to you this package and that you needed to follow the instructions for your own safety. He said to tell you that you weren't safe with that man you're with."

"Where is this package?"

She stands and ruffles through her drawers to return with a yellow manila envelope. She hands it to me, and I take another quick look at the door before opening it. The first thing I pull out is a note.

*Willow,*

*I know I don't deserve your trust, but I need it right now. You're in serious danger. You have something they want, and you don't even know it. I need to see you. They will never stop coming for you. Contact me on the number enclosed as soon as you receive this. Don't tell Johnny about me. He's using you to get this information. I know you think he's back with good intentions, but he isn't. I made the mistake of telling him you have what he's looking for, that's why he came back. I hope you trust me enough to know I did what I did to protect you. Call me as soon as you can.*

*Dad*

I lower the letter, hands trembling. He hasn't bothered to contact me for years, but he can manage a note when it suits him. And he wants me to trust him? Can I trust him? Can I trust any of them? I'm starting to think I haven't even scratched the surface of whatever it is that's going on here. I lower the note and look to my mother, who is staring at me with wide eyes.

"I will deal with this," I say. "Don't worry yourself about it anymore."

"Who is Johnny?"

Of course she read it.

"It doesn't matter, it's not safe for you to know anymore."

"Of course you don't trust me," she mutters, crossing her arms, "You'll never forgive me, will you?"

"You tried to kill me."

Her eyes narrow. "You don't understand, I was trying to save you."

I can't hear this. Not again.

"I have to go," I say, standing. "It was nice to see you."

Sarah enters the room, cutting off her reply.

"It's time for some afternoon swimming," She announces.

She's saving me.

Like she always does.

I stand and shove the envelope into my bag before zipping it up. I hug my mother briefly.

"I'll talk with you soon."

"We're not finished here, Willow," she warns, eyes locked onto mine.

I look from her to Sarah and back again. "Yes, we are."

I leave the room and wait for Sarah at the exit. She gives me a sympathetic squeeze on the shoulder, and I hug her once more before leaving and going back to the truck where Jagger is waiting, face expressionless, eyes narrowed. He's always on alert. Always watching. Always waiting for the next attack.

I wonder what it's like to live like that.

"You ok?"

He asks the question the moment I'm in the truck.

"I'm fine."

"Is your mom good?"

"Sure."

"Don't believe you," he mutters.

"I'm fine, Jagger. Seriously."

I glance out the window as he reverses out of the parking lot. I'm fighting the tears, but mostly, I'm fighting the confusion. Is what my dad said true? Is Jagger only here because he wants whatever it is I apparently have? I don't want to believe it's true, but would I be stupid to not even consider it?

I don't know.

I don't know anything.

"What the fuck happened in there?" Jagger asks as we drive back towards my house.

"I just don't like visiting her, Jagger. That's it."

"You're lyin' to me."

I don't look at him.

"Can we just go home?"

He exhales, more frustrated than anything. "Look, I don't know what's goin' on, but you can trust me. You know that, right?"

I look to him now, the envelope burning a hole in my bag. The letter looming in my mind. "Can I?"

He pulls the truck over, turning to face me. "What's that supposed to mean?"

"If you didn't need my father so badly, would you have come back?"

He studies me for a moment, his eyes scanning over my face. Then he leans in, gripping my chin. "You know the answer to that. You know I want you. What more do you want me to say?"

"That you're not just here to get what you want and then you'll leave…"

He frowns. "You think I'd bother protecting you if that's all I wanted? I'd let Manchez get hold of you and I'd just get the information from him. I'm protectin' you because you matter, Willow."

I swallow.

He makes a valid point.

My father was the one who lied to me.

What reason do I have to trust him?

None.

"Things are complicated," Jagger goes on, "I get that, but I'm not here because anyone forced me to be. I'm here because I want to be."

I don't know why…I just believe him.

I trust that he's telling the truth.

"Yeah," I say, leaning in to press my forehead against his. "I know. Sorry, my mom gets me all crazy."

"You're not her, you know?"

I pull back and look at him. "I know."

"I see you, Willow. I see the things you don't want me to see, and I know you're not her."

I lean in and he wraps an arm around me.

"I got you," he murmurs.

His words hit me where they need to, and I can't find it in my heart to do anything else but trust him. He might be dangerous, he might be hard and beautiful all at the same time, but he's mine and that alone is enough to make me hang on. I don't know if the next month will hold agony, or if I'll wake up one day and realize this was all fake, but I can sure as hell give it the best I have while it's good. I take his hand and bring his fingertips to my lips.

He's got me.

~*~*~*~*

"Dude, you're cheating!" I yell, tossing a poker chip at Angel.

He snorts a laugh. "Take it off, Willow. Rules are rules."

We're playing strip poker. We drank a little too much, and somehow ended up here. I guess we were all restless, sick of being stuck inside and so we decided to make the most of it. Even Jenny and Ava joined in without fuss. So far, I'm down to my shirt and panties, and Ava is down to her bra and panties. Jenny is fully clothed, I don't know how, but man she's good at this.

Jagger is shirtless, and oh my, what a sight. Angel is down to his boxers and that too, is a sight to see. Ace is fully clothed.

The girls are losing this battle. Well, Ava and I are, anyway.

Jenny is a sly dog, and her and Ace are going head-to-head to be the last to have to remove their clothes. I stand up with a huff, and my head swims just a touch. Damn Jagger and his whiskey.

I wink at Angel and give Jagger my best grin. Then I start wiggling my hips and removing my shirt, button by button, in slow motion. The men whistle and Jagger gives me a look that promises sweet revenge later. I slowly remove the shirt from my body and toss it at Angel, who whoops with delight. Jagger grips my hips and pulls me towards him, sliding his tongue around my belly button ring as my stomach presses against his mouth.

"If you get naked, and my boys get to see this beautiful body, it won't end well…"

"Oh?" I grin, gripping his chin and leaning down to kiss him.

"Ugh, you two get a room!" Jenny yells, laughing.

"Not until you're naked sister," I say, pulling away from Jagger.

She throws her head back and gives her best evil laugh. "Ace will be naked first."

"Like fuck," Ace grins, throwing down his cards. "Royal flush. Get them off, beautiful!"

Jenny groans and tosses her cards at him. He roars with laughter, and I watch as my sister stands and removes her top, stopping Ace in his tracks. His eyes widen, and he looks at Jenny in a way that makes even my legs tremble. God, he wants her. He wants her so damned bad. I laugh and plonk down onto my seat, shooting another whiskey shot.

That's when everything changes.

It happens quickly, so quickly it takes me a moment to realize something is wrong. I hear glass breaking, and then I see Jagger leap to his feet and start yelling. I don't click as to what he's saying until he has me in his arms, his hand is planted firmly over my mouth. I struggle, unsure what's happening. My eyes dart to the left and I see Ace and Angel are covering Ava and Jenny's mouths, too.

Jagger drags me down the hall and into the bathroom, and the other men follow. They shove us in and let us go, all of them looking so wound up it's terrifying. Jagger pulls all the towels from the racks and shoves them onto the floor, jamming the gap under the door as much as he can. I gasp and grip the sink, steadying myself. "What's happening? Jagger? What's going on?"

"Chemical bomb," he growls, stuffing the towels so far under the door cracks, "someone just threw one through the kitchen window. We gotta get out. If it gets into your lungs, you'll pass out."

"What?" I cry, confused. "Who threw it?"

"Manchez. He's tryin' to get hold of you. He's clever. So fuckin' smart. He knows where we are now."

"Oh God, I don't feel so…" Jenny begins, then her eyes roll back, and she passes out. Ace catches her in his arms.

"One down boss," he mutters, glancing at the bathroom window. "What do we do?"

"They'll be waiting. Angel, go and get our guns and our clothes. Cover your mouth, hold your breath."

Angel nods and puts a towel over his mouth, then rushes out. I turn to Jagger, who is now staring out the window, too.

"Where does this go?" he asks me.

"Out into the back area. There's a gate that leads out onto the street."

"We need to get you girls out."

"But…."

"There's no other choice."

Angel returns with the guns and our clothes. Jagger takes the gun, making sure it's loaded, then he peers out the window. We quickly dress ourselves and we cover Jenny as best we can.

"Is she going to be okay?" I ask Ace as he scoops her back into his arms.

"Yeah, she should be."

Should be?

"I think they're around front," Jagger mutters. "Chances are they'll barge in in a matter of minutes."

"Do we get them now boss?" Angel asks.

"No, it's too risky. It's a public street. We just need to get the girls out of here. Take them to a random hotel, pay with cash. At least until we can figure something out."

Angel nods and pulls the window open. He gets out first and I wait anxiously to hear if gun shots will fire off. My stomach twists as I wait, anxiously, praying we don't hear a single thing. I take Ava's hand and squeeze, she's white as a ghost. Ace adjusts Jenny then climbs out next, followed by Ava. I look to Jagger, and he gives me a nod.

"Are you coming?"

"I'll be there."

"Jagger, I need my handbag," I say quickly, suddenly remembering the information in there.

The information my father left me.

If they find that…

"What for?"

"It contains some, ah, information about my mother. If they get hold of it…"

"Where is it?"

"On the kitchen counter."

"I'll get it. Just get out of here."

"What about you?"

"I'll be fine. Go."

He shoves me towards the window before I can say another word. Angel grips me around the waist the moment I'm halfway out and pulls me quickly into the dark. My heart is racing, and my mind keeps returning to Jagger. What if he doesn't get out? What if they kill him?

"Will he be ok?" I ask Angel as we move to safety.

"He can handle himself. Don't speak again, Willow. It's crucial we get out of here alive."

I don't say another word as Angel leads us behind some bushes and then peers out. He scans the streets around us, and his eyes fall on the car parked over the road from the apartment.

"They're watching. We can't get out this way. Are there any other exits?"

I nod and point to the other side of the yard where a small fence joins our place to the neighbors. "If we climb into their yard and go over their fence, there is a big open field on the other side. We can get out that way."

Angel nods and we begin quietly shuffling out. After a huge struggle to get over the fence with a passed-out Jenny, we finally manage to get into the field. We hurry across it and take some back streets into town, until we can safely flag down a taxi. When we get in, Angel watches behind us to make sure we aren't being followed, then he gives instructions to a hotel.

We drive in silence for what feels like hours, but really, it's no more than half an hour at the most. Jenny is stirring on and off, Ava is staring blankly out the window and my mind keeps going back to Jagger. What if something happened to him? What if he thought we went out the other side of the yard and got shot? I fight back my panic and feel a rough hand reach over and squeeze mine. I glance at Ace, who is staring at me.

"He'll be fine."

"What if they got him?"

"He'll be fine…"

We arrive at a small, secluded hotel and check in. Then, we all quietly sit for a few hours, all of us scared, all of us wondering what happened. During that time Jenny wakes up groggily and we encourage her to drink lots of water and rest. We have three rooms, but they're connected, so we tuck Jenny into the bed in one and we wait with the guys in Angel and Ace's room. I'm sitting in a chair, just staring at the window, when we hear the pounding on the door. I leap to my feet, but Angel grips my arm, stopping me.

"Wait here."

He takes his gun and walks over, peering through the hole. A moment later he swings the door open and Jagger steps in. He's covered in blood and pale. Anxiety grips my chest as I rush towards him.

"You're hurt," I say, reaching for him.

"It's just a graze," he snaps, shoving past me as he walks into the room.

I step back. Shaking.

"You good, brother?" Ace asks.

"Get the first-aid kit out of the car and I'll patch it up," Jagger mutters, sitting on a chair and leaning forward.

"Manchez?" Angel murmurs, crossing his arms.

He nods sharply. "He shot at me."

"Are you ok?" I try again.

"Fine," he grunts.

He's angry at me.

It's written all over his face.

Maybe he's just shaken up.

Perhaps I need to back off.

"I guess we'll call it a night," I say, carefully.

Jagger doesn't even look in my direction.

What the hell happened?

# 15

I hesitate for a good long time before finally disappearing out of the room and into the one I'm supposed to be sharing with Jagger. I'm not sure how that'll go, considering he is making it very clear he wants nothing to do with me. I disappear into the shower for about twenty minutes, taking the time to wash my hair, shave my legs and try to turn my brain off. When I get out, I pull just a shirt on and then sit on the end of the bed. Jagger comes in just as I'm about to turn and crawl into the sheets. He glares at me, his shoulder is patched up and his jeans are still bloody.

He's holding my bag in his hand and he tosses it onto the floor before storming over and gripping my face, shocking me. He brings his lips down over mine hard and fast, frustration pouring from him. I groan when he shoves me back on the bed, flattening me with his hard body. One free hand slides up my thighs and finds bare pussy. I groan as he bites my neck and slides his fingers into me, thrusting them in a way that makes my back arch.

"Jagger…" I whimper.

He doesn't say anything, and I notice his body is tense and wound up. If he needs me right now, I'll say nothing. Perhaps this is just how he deals with these situations. I choose not to say anything and just go with the flow. I need him. I want to feel every part of him over me right now. Being away from him…it scared me. His lips are hot and soft, and they move against mine with desperation while he struggles with his sore arm to free his jeans.

I reach down and push his hand out of the way, and I undo his button before shoving his jeans down his hips. I can feel his cock, hard and hot against my hand as it springs out. He discards his jeans and goes back to kissing and tormenting me, his fingers grazing over my nipples and his lips teasing mine. He edges my legs apart, and probes my entrance, before sliding inside me.

I groan and arch as he fills me slowly. He makes a ragged grunting sound and uses his one free arm to prop himself up as he begins rocking his hips in and out. I whimper and my eyes fall closed as his cock slides in and out, stroking the sensitive flesh that's wound so tightly inside me. When I open my eyes, he's watching me, his blue gaze cold as ice.

It's terrifying.

"Are you mine, Willow?" he growls.

"What?" I whimper as he slowly slides his length out and gently pushes it back in, inch by inch.

"You heard me. Are you mine?"

"Yes," I gasp.

"Are you honest with me, Willow?" The way he just said my name has my skin prickling.

He jerks his hips, bringing me closer to the edge. I cry out and bite my lip, desperate to feel my release. It's so close, so dammed close.

"Answer me!" he barks.

"Oh…" I gasp, as my release hangs on the edge.

"Don't you cum," he roars, "this isn't for you."

He pulls his cock out and his body leaves mine so quickly it takes me a second to get my head around whatever the fuck just happened. My release dies just as quickly as it began, and I'm panting with frustration. My eyes go to him, and I watch as he falls back onto the bed taking his cock into his hand, jerking it hard and fast. His eyes lock onto mine, and right now I have no idea what the hell is happening. He grunts and I gasp as semen shoots from his cock in waves, landing on his stomach.

"Liar…" he seethes as he jerks the last of his release from his body.

Liar? What is he talking about? I stare at him, confused. I sit up and shuffle to the end of the bed, staring down at the floor. I see it then. The envelope laying open on the ground, having fallen from my bag when he threw it. He knows. *He knows*. That's why he's so angry. That's what is making him act like this.

"It's not what you think," I say, shaking my head and turning towards him.

"Bullshit."

I stand and pull on my clothes. I'm not doing this now. No.

"My mother only gave it to me today. I didn't know what it was," I say as I do up my pants.

"You're a god damned liar," he barks, standing and using a towel to swipe at the semen on his stomach.

"I didn't lie to you, Jagger. I just didn't tell you," I mutter.

"Do you know what could have happened to you tonight if Manchez had gotten hold of you? Do you have any fuckin' idea how close you came to losing your life?"

"I know!" I scream, throwing my hands up.

"No, you don't fuckin' know. I could have avoided all that if you had told me about that fuckin' note."

"Oh, what a load of crap. The note changes nothing," I growl. "Manchez still would have done what he did tonight."

"You don't fuckin' trust me. I have wasted my time and effort trying to make you see I'm not the bad guy in all this. What information do you have that your father is talking about? Tell me. Tell me what the fuck you're hiding!"

"I'm hiding nothing!" I bellow, hot tears threatening to burst free.

"Stop lying!"

I reach down and take my bag, hurling it over my shoulder. How dare he. His eyes are like fire, and he's glaring at me with such anger it makes me sick to my stomach.

"You stole me Jagger," I seethe, voice trembling. "You fucking stole me and upended my life. None of this was on me and I never wanted a god damned thing to do with it."

He storms over, and I wearily take a few steps back, hands going out in front of me.

"You're still holdin' onto the fact that I took you. Ever thought that I did you a fuckin' favor?"

"Because you wanted the information, too. Don't you pretend it had anything to do with protecting me."

"It didn't, but it came to be the only thing that mattered," he rasps, frustration in his tone.

"I don't fucking matter to you…"

"We are still doing this. You just can't let it go, can you? You just refuse to believe I care. You lied to me, you kept information that you know could have helped. You did that because you don't trust me."

"I barely had a chance to look at it. God damn. Fuck you, Jagger," I yell so loudly my throat hurts.

Angel busts into the room and doesn't seem to notice or care that Jagger is butt naked.

"You two need to stop," he hisses, "we can hear you a mile away!"

"Oh. We're stopping," I say, turning and walking towards the door.

"You do not fucking leave," Jagger warns.

I have a moment to get out the front door and run before he gets his jeans on. I need to get out of here. I can't deal with this right now. I rush out the front door, and flag down a taxi. Thankfully, one stops right away. I leap in and tell him to take me as far away from this hotel as possible. He drives away just as Jagger comes running out the door. My phone begins ringing almost instantly. I ignore it. Screw him. Screw all of this.

He wants to treat me like a god damned dog, fine.

I'll leave.

I turn my phone on silent and notice the messages flashing on the screen over and over.

Jagger: Get the fuck back here. It's dangerous. Do you have any idea the danger you just put yourself in?

Ava: Where are you? Please come back. Jagger is beside himself. He is going crazy. He said Manchez could get hold of you. Swallow your pride and come back, please?

Jagger: Fucking answer the damned phone.

I swallow back my tears and switch the phone off. I need to find a payphone. I want answers and I want them now. I'm sick of living under this constant shadow of fear. It's not fair. I tell the taxi driver to take me to a payphone and he stops about twenty minutes down the road. I get out and then pay him. Then, I go to the phone. I'm not using my cell for this. I'm using a phone that can't be traced back. I pull my father's note from my bag and dial the number.

"Willow?"

How does he know it's me?

"How did you know it was me?" I ask, voice shaky.

"You're the only person I gave this number to," he explains, and his familiar voice puts a pang of pain into my chest. I hate that he's done this to me. To us.

"What do you want?"

"We need to talk. Where can we meet?"

"You really think I'm going to trust you?" I laugh, bitterly.

"I'm not out to hurt you. You're my daughter. I have done wrong, Willow, but I'm not going to do anything to endanger you."

"Oh, really? Then why the hell am I here? It's all because of you.

"We don't have time for this. You're in serious danger if you stay with Jagger."

"Jagger hasn't hurt me."

"He's using you. It's all going to blow up in your face. Please, we need to talk."

I ignore that. "Why did you give me that note and what information do I supposedly have?"

"I hid some information in something you own."

"Seriously?" I shake my head, closing my eyes. "And you're here telling me you're trying not to endanger me. That shit right there is why I'm in trouble."

"I had no choice."

"You're as selfish as you always were."

"Please, just listen to me."

"I have nothing to say to you. You either tell me what the hell is going on or I'm hanging up and you'll never hear from me again."

"There's going to be a massive bust," he says quickly.

"What sort of bust?"

"The information I gave you is crucial. You can't let anyone have it. I need you to set Jagger up with fake information and have him meet Manchez at a location specified by me. Both will be taken down there."

"No." I say, simply.

"What?"

"I said no. I won't do it."

"Jagger is lying to you, Willow. Why won't you listen!"

"I'm going now."

"Willow!"

I hang up and slide my back down the wall of the payphone, cupping my face in my hands. I gasp and then cry until my body trembles and shakes. They say everything in life happens for a reason, right now I just can't see that reason.

I just can't see it.

~*~*~*~

I find a run-down motel and pay for a room with cash. When I get into the old, smelly room, I sigh. This is going to be a long night. I throw my bag down and fall onto the springy bed. I pull out my phone and read the messages. I feel bad for Jenny and Ava, I know how worried they'll be, but I need to get my bearings. I feel like I've got whiplash. Like the world is just crashing down around me.

Jagger: Baby please. Call me.

Baby? The man has a personality disorder. Seriously.

Ava: Please tell me you're ok? I'm sick with worry.

I text Ava back quickly.

Willow: I'm ok. Just need some time. Tell Jagger I'm fine.

She responds right away.

Ava: He's gone out looking for you. He's so worried honey, please come back.

Willow: I can't right now, please understand. I'm safe. I promise. X

Ava: Stay safe, I love you x

Willow: You too.

Jagger: Where are you?

I sigh, feeling awfully overwhelmed right now.

My phone rings once again and I angrily open it knowing he won't stop until I answer it.

"What?"

"Where are you?" He sounds worn out and he's panting.

"I'm fine. You need to leave me be."

"Do you have any fuckin' idea how much danger you're in?"

"I wish I cared," I mutter.

"Willow, fuckin' hell. You don't have to talk to me, but you need protection, at least accept that."

"Then send Angel or Ace over. I don't want to see you."

He's silent a long moment. "Fuck. Fuck. Fine. Answer when they call."

I hang up without another word and a moment later my phone rings again. I answer and hear Angel's voice come across the line.

"Where are you?"

I give him the location.

"I'll be there soon."

"Ok."

I hang up the phone and hope Jagger doesn't come with him. Regardless of what I said, I do value my safety, so I know having Angel around will be a good thing. My head is spinning, so I go and wash my face before getting myself a drink of water and sitting on the old, run-down chair. I stare at the door, praying he shows up alone. Soon, a knock sounds out.

I get up and open the door and see Angel standing. Alone. Thank God. He gives me a kind smile, which I'm truly grateful for. I know he doesn't have to be here, in fact, it's probably the last place he wants to be but here he is, doing me a favor when I probably don't deserve one. I wave my arm towards the seat, and he walks in, sitting down.

"I'm sorry," I mumble, feeling a whole lot stupid right now.

"You have every reason to be angry, but you gotta know that running off isn't helping."

"He hurt me."

Angel nods. "I know he did, but Jagger doesn't think sometimes."

"It's not an excuse…" I mutter, feeling defensive.

"Look, I know what he's like, but I also saw him tonight. He cares about you, a lot. I know you can't let go, I know he took you and for a while your life was all but pleasant. I know that can't be easily forgotten, but in a sense, he was doing you a favor."

"Why do you all keep throwing that in my face?" I snap. "It's all I hear, over and over again. Like I should be grateful he turned my life upside down."

"I'm not throwing it in your face, I'm just stating the obvious and that is that you would have been taken no matter what. Jagger can be hard, and his life isn't rosy and sweet, but he's not a bad person. He's been through more than you could ever imagine in his short life. He saved you, even if you refuse to see it like that. If you want to blame someone, blame your dad…"

"You think I don't?"

"Then why are you so hostile towards Jagger?"

"You don't get it, do you?"

"No, I don't. I can't understand why you're refusing to let this go."

"I'm in love with him, Angel," I yell, the words shocking even me. I've thought them, God have I thought them, but I've never said them out loud. "I hate it, but I fucking love him. It's sick, it's twisted, and it's based on a foundation that is so dangerous I know it'll break…"

"He's in love with you, too."

I grunt.

"Give him a chance and you might just see it. We're not bad people, you know."

"You're all in a gang," I point out with a small, weak smile.

"I'd prefer to call us a dark brotherhood."

I huff, and my smile gets a little more genuine. "The dark brothers."

He smiles.

"Thank you, for being here."

He stands and stares down at me. "It's no problem. I'm goin' to crash on the couch. Get some rest."

I nod and force myself to stand. With wobbly legs, I take myself to bed.

My heart confused.

My mind a mess.

My body tired.

# 16

The next morning, Angel and I go back to the hotel as soon as we wake. When we get in, no one is there, not a single sign of life. Angel tries to call Jagger, but his phone is playing up and continually dies. I try on my phone, but nobody answers. We both become uneasy. I had a few missed calls from Jagger early this morning, but being as stubborn as I was, I didn't answer them and turned my phone off. *I turned my phone off.* What the fuck is wrong with me?

Angel swears and curses as he tries to get his phone to work, all while giving me one of those concerned looks and then hesitantly drives us back to the apartment. The moment we arrive, Angel tells me to stay in the car and does a quick sweep of the place before coming out to tell me that Jenny and Ava are home. Alone.

I'm a little more than confused.

Rushing out of the car, I go inside, desperate for answers.

"Jagger left early this morning after a phone call," Jenny explains the second she sees my expression. "Ace went with him. They told us to lock the doors and left us with a few guns. That's all I know. He didn't take his phone. He rushed out so quickly we didn't know what was going on."

"Why the fuck would he leave you girls alone?" Angel growls, looking around.

"He went quickly. Something was off."

Angel uses my phone to ring Ace, no answer either. He then calls Rusty and Bull, who are both back at Jagger's old place. They tell him they haven't heard from Jagger, and he isn't there. With every passing second, I can feel my heart lodging into my throat.

"Stay here," Angel announces, slamming my phone down. "Shut and lock the doors, if anyone comes, you call the police. I don't care. Just call them. I'm going to find Jagger."

He's leaving us alone.

Angel hands me a gun, and I take the heavy, cold object. He does one more sweep of the place and then rushes out the door. I turn to Jenny and Ava, who both look equally as scared. For Jagger to leave us alone...it doesn't seem right. I lock the doors, then double check them all. My phone rings from my bag and I rush over, pulling it out to see an unknown number flashing across my screen.

"Hello?"

"Willow, it's me."

It's my father. How the hell did he get my number?

"How did you get my number?" I demand.

"It doesn't matter. You need to listen to me. Jagger is in trouble."

"What?"

"I called him this morning and made a deal with him. If he let you go and let you live your life without involvement, I'd tell him where Manchez was. They're making a huge deal down at the wharf today and it's going to be massive. Jagger is going down there. He wants to end this. He agreed."

He agreed to let me go.

For information?

I feel sick to my stomach as I clamp my eyes shut.

"What have you done?" I whisper into the phone.

"There is something else. They are going to make a massive bust. It's going to be a blood bath, Willow. It's going to end badly. If you want to save him, you're going to need to stop him but only I can tell you how to do that."

"What have you done?" I scream again, and Ava comes up beside me, gripping my arm and squeezing.

"You need to find him, but if I'm going to tell you where, you need to get something for me," he goes on.

"I don't need to do anything for you!" I yell. "You've ruined my life."

"Do you want Jagger alive?" he growls.

I close my eyes. I need to stay calm. If I'm going to do this, I need to stay calm.

"Yes." I answer simply.

"In your old dressing table, the one you had as a child, there is information. If you bust open the bottom, you'll find it."

God damn him.

"What information?"

"It doesn't matter. Go and get it. Right now."

I put the phone on speaker and turn, running into my room. I toss the old dresser over, even though it's my favorite, and things go flying. Jenny and Ava follow me, asking what's going on, but I ignore them. I use my foot to kick, over and over, until the base of it just falls off. Weak. Resecured in a way that could only happen if someone was in a hurry. How did I miss that? I lean down and pull the timber away. Inside there are papers in a plastic wrap. I pull them out and quickly read over them. It's just a bunch of co-ordinates.

That's it?

"What is this?" I demand.

"It's co-ordinates to an island where the biggest drug deals this side of the world happen. It is some of the most hidden information and if it gets into the wrong hands, things will turn very bad."

God, I feel sick.

"What am I supposed to do with this?"

"Bring it to me."

"Why?"

"If the cops find you with that it's going to be very bad for you. If Jagger gets hold of it, it'll be very dangerous. I'm the only person who can have it, Willow. I need it and I need it now."

This is blackmail. My own father is using me.

"I don't know…"

"If you love him. You'll bring me that. Then I'll tell you how to find him before he gets his life taken from him. The choice is yours. Bring those to me on the corner of South and Martin in twenty minutes. Come alone."

"Fine."

I hang up the phone and stand, running into the office. Ava and Jenny run after me.

"What's happening?" Ava demands.

"Dammit, Willow, who was that?" Jenny asks.

"Jagger is in trouble. I need to find him," I answer, ruffling around.

Jenny shakes her head. "How?"

"I don't know yet. I need to do something first. Then I'm going to find him. You two stay here."

"Fuck no," Ava shakes her head.

"Ava," I say, grabbing her shoulders. "I don't have time to argue with you right now. Please, if you care about me, you'll stay here."

"Willow," she goes to argue, but I pull away.

I throw the papers into the photocopier and photocopy them. This information is crucial and there is no way in hell that I'm giving my father it back without copying it first. He might think he has one up on me, but he's about to find out he's very wrong.

"Wrap these in plastic," I say, handing them to Jenny. "Hide them so good nobody will ever find them."

"What are they?"

"Just do as I say."

I pull on my shoes and some dark shades, and then I shove the papers into my handbag and rush to the front door. I pick up the gun and put it down my pants.

"Willow," Ava calls, running after me. "I'm not letting you go alone."

"You don't get a choice," I say, glancing at her. "Just please, stay here. If I don't come back, call the police."

"Willow," she yells.

I hug her and Jenny, then I turn and rush out the front door to the sounds of their yelling.

I have to do this.

I have to.

~*~*~*~

I see my father as soon as I step out of the cab, he's standing off the footpath near an old, abandoned building, alone.

His eyes move to me the moment I get out and when the cab driver is gone, he steps towards me, glancing around. He's showing no emotion, no sign of the love he once felt for me. He was my hero and now he's looking at me like he's never even heard my name.

My heart breaks a little.

"Let's save any chit chat," I say before he gets the chance to speak. "You wanted the information, you got it. Now tell me where Jagger is."

I thrust the papers at him, and he looks down, flicking through them before tucking them into his jacket and looking at me.

"You won't find him."

"Excuse me?"

"I'm sorry, Willow."

What is going on?

What's happening?

He closes his eyes and sighs. "I'm sorry to have to do this to you, but I really had no other choice. I didn't tell Jagger where to find Manchez, I told him that Manchez had taken Maggie and if he wanted her back, where to find her. I set him up. I had no option. As soon as he arrives there, he'll die."

No.

No.

"How could you?" I scream, taking a step back, staring at the man who is supposed to love me.

"I need Jagger out of the way. He has been a thorn in my side for too long. He wouldn't step away. I had no choice. This isn't about you. This goes far deeper than you could ever imagine. I had to do this. I knew Jagger would take you to get to me, and I knew he would eventually fall for you, how could he not? It worked out exactly how I needed it to."

I'm going to be sick.

All along my father was one step ahead of Jagger. All along he was behind this.

"How could you? I'm your daughter," I whisper as tears burst forth and roll down my cheeks.

"I never intended for you to get hurt. I did what I had to do to get him out of the picture. It had to happen like this."

"You're working with Manchez," I say, shaking my head in horror as I angrily swipe a tear away.

"Yes."

How could I be so stupid?

How could I have let this happen?

"Please, just let him go."

He shakes his head, pulling out his gun just as a car rolls in and stops beside us, the windows dark. "Get in the car."

My eyes widen as fear grips my chest. "Dad, please."

"Look, just do as I ask, and no one will get hurt. Get in the car."

"Dad…"

"Now. Willow."

I slide into the car, trembling. The drive is a man I've never seen before, and he stares straight ahead as my father gets in beside me, reaching over and jerking my hands forward so he can cuff them. I fight, God do I fight, but it's no use. With one swift slap, he renders me speechless and utterly broken.

"I don't want to hurt you," he grinds out, "stop fighting me. As soon as he's out of the picture, you can go back to your life. Do you understand?"

I don't say anything, I refuse to acknowledge him at all. As far as I'm concerned, he's dead to me. We drive for about twenty minutes and pull up at an old, run-down warehouse. My father pulls me out of the car and drags me inside and into a secured room. I go numbly, not saying a single word, but vowing to myself that he will pay for this.

With blood.

After a few minutes the door to the room opens and Manchez steps in. I'd recognize that face anywhere. He smirks and walks forward, running a finger over my cheek, I jerk my head away.

"Lovely to see you again, Willow."

"I delivered on my end," my father says, "you deliver on yours. Don't hurt her."

"I don't intend on hurting her, at least, not if she behaves. Now tell me, sweet Willow, where are Jagger's little gang friends?"

They're still not with him?

That gives me a hope I didn't know I needed.

"I don't know."

He laughs lightly and cracks his knuckles. "Don't lie to me. You won't like how it ends."

"I don't know," I grind out. "When I got back this morning, they were all gone."

His eyes meet my father's, and they share a short nod.

"Very well. Kane, make sure she's tied up good. We'll finish this my way. Did you get what I needed?"

My father hands him the papers and Manchez smiles. "Well done, my boy."

What the fuck is this?

"You're fucked," I growl, kicking out and just missing my father.

Manchez grins and has the nerve to look proud of that fact. "Well, I think that's the nicest thing anyone has ever said to me."

"You won't get away with this," I grind out. "Jagger is smarter than you."

He laughs now. "He's going to die, Willow. I promise you that. In fact, he'll be arriving right where I need him shortly."

I close my eyes and swallow. I have to get out of here. I have to do something.

"Deal with her, Kane, and then meet me in the den. We leave in half an hour. We need to make sure we're prepared."

When Manchez leaves, I stare at my father. Is he my only hope? My only chance at stopping this. I have to try.

"Daddy, please, don't hurt him. I love him."

For the first time, my father's face softens a touch.

"I have to do this. I'm sorry."

"You've been in love before, haven't you?" I cry. "Please don't take that from me."

"It all ends eventually," he mutters. "All of it."

"I'm your daughter."

His eyes are pained as he fiddles with the ropes on the chair, when he's secured me, he removes the handcuffs and steps back. He avoids my gaze for a moment, before making his eyes emotionless and looking at me.

"I'm sorry I let you down. But this is how it has to be."

"Dad!" I cry as he leaves the room.

I hang my head and scream, my back aches and my wrists burn as I tug at the ropes. I curse and tug until I hear the cars pulling out of the driveway.

I know there will be someone guarding my door. I yank again, only this time I notice they rope is a little looser than normal.

My father did them quite tight to begin with so why are they loose now? I keep pulling and yanking until my wrists are bleeding, but the binds are coming undone.

Another hour of pulling and burning, and I manage to free myself. Did he do them like that on purpose? Was my father helping me? Or was it just an error on his part? I don't have time to ponder it. I stare around the room, it's empty and there's nothing I can use as a weapon. Except the chair I was sitting on. I flip it over and quickly kick one of the heavy wooden legs, breaking it off. The door opens just as I pick it up, and a man steps through. His eyes widen when he sees that I'm free.

I swing before he can raise his gun, connecting with his head and sending him stumbling backwards. I hit him again and again, blood spattering across my face, until he lies unconsciously on the floor. I pick up his gun and tuck it into my pants, and then I rush out of the room and through the warehouse that, as far as I can tell, is empty. I dig around until I find a pair of keys and then I rush out the front door.

That's when I hear a voice. I spin around and see a man standing just outside the door, glaring at me.

I fumble quickly for my gun, praying I don't kill him but in this moment, not caring if I do or not.

I point it at his chest and shoot, sending him stumbling backwards. He hits the ground with a thud and makes a gurgled sound. I turn and run, not looking back.

I have to find Jagger.

If I don't, he's going to die.

# 17

I drive until I can find a phone, and I call Ava's number, the only one I know off by heart. The moment she answers, I frantically tell her everything that has happened. She informs me that Angel is back and that he couldn't find Jagger. Bull and Rusty are out looking. I demand that Angel gets on the phone and the moment he answers, I tell him everything I know.

"They've led him to the wharf," I finish on a gasp. "They told him they have Maggie."

"Fuck!" Angel barks. "Get here. Hurry."

I hang up and get back into the truck, making it back to the apartment in a very short amount of time. Angel is out the front and the moment he sees me, he leaps into the car and hands me a gun before ordering me to drive.

"Tell me what's happening?" I plead, my hands trembling.

"They're leading him to the wharf, when he arrives, they'll kill him."

"Why would he go without all of you?" I ask, confused. "Why would he just leave and try to save her alone?"

"I don't fuckin' know," Angel growls. "Your dad must have said something to convince him to come without backup."

Dammit.

Dammit.

We drive to the wharf and the moment we arrive, Angel tells me where to go so we're hidden. Then, we both slowly get out of the car. Angel instructs me to stay right here because it isn't safe. After much arguing back and forth, I agree just to get him off my back. Then, he disappears. As soon as he's gone, I pull the gun out I still have, and I tiptoe down to a line of trees and crouch behind them. I peer out and see a lineup of black cars down at the Wharf entrance.

It's Manchez.

I crawl closer and I hear the sounds of more cars coming in.

God, please don't be Jagger.

I'm just about to make a run for a line of shipping containers when a hand goes around my mouth from behind. I kick and struggle, but I can't get out of the vice like grip. A voice fills my ears, and I shudder. It's Manchez. "Did you honestly think you could outsmart me? Stupid girl."

He crushes my mouth with his hand and drags me down towards the group of cars. I can only pray Angel notices. God, please notice. My father meets my frantic stare as he stands beside a black SUV, and his eyes widen. I kick and squirm, but a fist drives into my ribs so hard I'm sent down to my knees, gasping for air.

"You said you wouldn't hurt her!" My father yells, trying to shove Manchez out of the way.

"Question me again, Kane, and I'll blow your fuckin' brains out."

My father takes a step back, his eyes meet mine and he looks like for a moment, he's sorry. I struggle for air, but mostly to keep calm and not give Manchez any further reason to hurt me. I'm not help if he hurts me. When I hear a car coming into the lot, terror explodes in my chest. *Jagger*. I see his car come into view and I know I have only seconds to come up with something or he'll die.

"Enjoy this Willow," Manchez grins, raising his gun. "He's about to be splattered all over his own windshield."

"I copied the information!" I cry, thinking quickly. "His members have it. If you kill him, they'll just use it. You're wasting your time."

Manchez lowers the gun and spins around, gripping me by the hair and hauling me off the ground, pulling me close to his face. "What did you say?"

"I didn't stutter," I gasp.

He spins me around and wraps an arm around my throat, pressing the gun to my temple. Jagger's car comes to a stop and when he gets out with Ace by his side, his face is ashen, and his eyes fall to me.

"Ah Jagger, just in time to see the show," Manchez grins.

"Let her go," he growls, confusion washing over his face, and I see the moment he realizes that he has been played.

"She just broke the news to me, you're smarter than I thought."

Jagger's eyes move to mine, and I plead with him to play along.

"She said you have a copy of the information and I'm going to need that back."

"You let her go or you'll get nothing."

Jagger takes a step forward.

Manchez tightens his arm around my throat, and I struggle to breathe.

"One more step, Jagger, and she's dead."

"Let her go," Jagger growls, his voice tight.

"Where is my information?" Manchez roars.

He squeezes so tightly my vision goes blurry, and then I hear the sound of a gun being fired.

Suddenly, I'm on the floor and Manchez is beside me, half his face blown off, bits of blood covering my face.

I retch and struggle to breathe as gun shots ring out al around me. I'm fighting against passing out and trying to get up. I manage to clear my vision just in time to see Angel, gun pointed at one of Manchez' men. He pulls the trigger, and the man falls to the ground.

The gunshots stop.

Then I hear Ace's pained voice.

"Jagger?"

I push to my feet and look over to see Jagger on the ground, his stomach bleeding. I rush over with shaky legs, dropping to the ground beside him.

"Jagger!" I yell, gripping his shoulders.

His eyes are closed and there's so much blood.

"Jagger!" I scream.

Angel leans down and checks his pulse. "He's still alive. We have to get him to a hospital, now."

"Jagger," I croak, shaking him. "Please wake up."

"Willow," Ace urges. "We have to go. The cops will be here any minute."

I turn and stare at the dead bodies lying around on the ground. Then I see my father, he's lying about two meters away, right near Manchez' dead body.

I force myself to my feet again and walk over. He's bleeding from the mouth and his body is jerking.

The gurgled sounds coming from his mouth is enough to have my entire body shutting down.

"Dad," I say, putting my hand on his face.

His eyes are fluttering, and they crack open, just a touch.

"Willow," he croaks.

"Dad, it's okay. It'll be okay."

"I'm sorry."

He gasps and then begins choking, blood pouring from his mouth.

"Dad!" I cry, taking his shoulders.

But it's too late.

He gasps again and then his breathing becomes shallow, the air slowly trickling away.

"Willow, we have to go," Ace urges.

"I can't leave him here," I yell, slapping my father lightly.

"He's going to die. He'll never make it. We have to go, or Jagger will die. The choice is yours."

The choice is mine.

I stare down at the man who brought me into this world, and the man who betrayed me in a way I'll never recover from.

"I'm sorry," I say as I lean down, kissing his cheek.

His body stops twitching.

The gasping fades away into silence.

There are no more sounds.

I know he's gone.

Ace pulls me to my feet as a pain I didn't think I'd feel crushes at my chest. Angel lifts Jagger, then we rush back to the truck and get in. I sit on the back seat, Jagger's head in my lap. His breathing is labored and he's as pale as a ghost. My tears fall onto his cheeks as I send a prayer up to the heavens.

"Please, don't you leave me. Jagger, please."

~*~*~*~

Jagger is whisked away as soon as we get into emergency. I'm taken to a room and put into a bed to get checked over. It turns out I have two broken ribs, and they want to run some scans to make sure I haven't punctured anything. I lay in the bed, numb and staring out the window. I think about my father, and all of the things I wish I could have said but didn't get a chance to. He's gone this time, really gone, and I'm not sure how I feel about that.

I hear voices soon after, and Jenny rushes into the room closely followed by Ava. I don't meet their gazes, I just stare blankly back down at my hands. They both crawl onto my bed, neither of them saying anything. They just hold onto me and when they do, the sobs break free, releasing all my emotions. When I finally fall into an exhausted sleep, they remain beside me. Like they always are.

Beside me.

I'm woken a few times after that for tests and scans, when I'm finally left to sleep, I don't wake until morning. When I move, my body aches and throbs. I open my eyes and instantly, my mind goes to Jagger. I sit up, groaning in pain and look around the room. Jenny is sitting on a chair beside the bed. My eyes meet hers and she stands, rushing over. She strokes a piece of hair from my face and smiles weakly.

"Jagger?"

"He's ok. He's in a bad way, but they think he'll make a full recovery."

My body slumps down and I shudder in relief.

"Do you want to see him?"

"Yes."

We call the nurse to do a check and give me the all clear to leave the room, then Jenny helps me out of bed. I'm sore, but other than a few fractures, I'll recover in a few days and be able to get on with life. It takes a little while to hobble out of the room, but as time passes, each step becomes easier. We get into an elevator and Jenny squeezes my hand.

"How are you feeling?"

"I'm ok, sore, but ok."

"I'm sorry about what happened out there yesterday."

I nod and chew on my bottom lip to keep the emotions from breaking out.

"I had so much I wanted to say to him," I whisper, in reference to our father.

She nods. She understands. "Me, too."

We stand in silence until we reach the intensive care unit. When we get out, Jenny leads me towards some rooms. We have to check we're allowed in, and when we're given permission, we step into one and I see Jagger in the third bed. I make a pained sound and he turns his head, meeting my gaze. Jenny leads me over to him, and I reach out and take his hand.

"Hey beautiful," he croaks.

"I'll leave you two to it."

Jenny slides a chair over and I sit on it, then she kisses my cheek and walks out. Jagger looks awful, his face is pale, and he's got tubes everywhere.

"You're ok…" I whisper.

"I'm ok."

"I'm so sorry all of that happened…"

He lightly shrugs. "It was going to happen sometime…"

I laugh even as a tear slides down my cheek. "Why are you always so calm?"

He reaches out, hanging onto my hand. "Calm is all I can be. We're goin' to be ok now. It's over."

"If I had lost you…" I whisper, glancing away.

"You didn't."

He's right. I didn't. But that doesn't stop the aching pain in my chest at the very thought of it.

"I'm sorry. For running out, for the fight, for everything that happened before all of this. I was acting like a child and I shouldn't have done that."

He glances at me. "Emotions were high, I can't blame you. It has been a fuckin' rough time."

"Is it really over now?"

He nods. "Manchez is dead. In the end, that's what the main goal was."

"The information?" I ask, choosing not to mention that I made a copy of it just yet.

"We'll figure something out. At least for now, I don't have to deal with him."

That's something, I suppose.

"The police, have they come by?" I ask, curious.

Jagger nods. "Yeah, but we are all giving the same story. Wrong place. Wrong time. We got caught up in something we shouldn't have. As far as they know, we had nothing to do with Manchez and what he had going down. Unless someone spills, they have nothing."

Thank God for that.

"What now?" I ask, scooting the chair closer. "What do we do?"

"Right now, I'm just glad everyone is safe. The rest of it I'll worry about later."

That's probably the best answer I've had in quite some time.

"My father was working for Manchez this entire time," I say, voice low. "He died out there."

Jagger nods. "I'm sorry. I know that isn't an easy piece of information to swallow. Especially with everything you've been through."

"Did you know?"

Jagger shakes his head. "No. I had suspicions after we caught him that something wasn't right, but I could have never picked that."

"Well," I murmur, staring at my hands. "At least he really is gone this time."

"Hey," he says, reaching for my hand and tugging it until I look up at him, "I got you."

He's got me.

Those words will always make something inside me feel a little safer.

Right now, that's what I need the most.

# 18

Jagger is released six days later, and I take him home to my place. I've spent the days that he's been in hospital, organizing my father's funeral. His actual funeral. One that he will really be buried during. My mother has obtained a day pass to come and attend with Sarah by her side. It's tomorrow and I feel sick in the stomach knowing I have to say goodbye. I don't know how I feel about it all and the thoughts are tormenting my mind.

I've had a lot of emotions about my father over the past week. I've been angry, sad, and confused. I'm angry that he did this to himself, and to our family. I'm sad because I lost him, without ever being able to ask him why, and I'm confused that I feel so many different emotions about one single person.

I walk into the bedroom where Jenny has set up a bed for Jagger. Angel is in with him, and they're discussing something. Jagger is looking much better, and his gunshot wound is healing well. When I enter, Angel stands and gives Jagger a swift nod.

"I'll leave you two. Yell out if you need anything, boss."

"Will do."

Angel smiles at me, and then leaves the room. I go over and sit on the edge of the bed, staring down at the man who has captured my soul.

"How you feelin' about tomorrow?" he asks.

I shrug, "Relieved. Confused. I don't know."

"Yeah, it's a big fuckin' mess."

"Also, there's something I didn't tell you…" I say, figuring now is the best time to tell him that I took the information before meeting my father.

His eyes narrow. "What?"

"I copied that information before I met with my father."

His eyes widen. "What?"

"I have it here."

"You're fuckin' clever, I knew you were," he grins, a smile I haven't seen from him in days.

"What's so important about this island anyway, other than it holding a lot of bad people?"

"That information could end some of the biggest drug trading in the world."

I raise my brows. "What?"

"I'll tell you all about it soon, but I need you to give it to me."

I hesitate. "I don't want any more danger."

"I know, but while that information is around, you're not safe. I need to get rid of it and make sure no one finds out you have it. They all need to think that Manchez had the only copy, and it went down with him."

He's right.

I have to trust him. Eventually, I have to give myself over to knowing he has my best interests at heart.

"Ok."

He takes my face into his hands and jerks me down towards him, kissing me. I groan and cling to him, sliding my tongue into his mouth and toying with his. God, I've missed this. Missed him.

"I need to fuck you so badly," he growls.

"You have a dirty mouth."

He licks my lower lip. "You love my dirty mouth."

"You have no idea. Tell me more."

He leans into my ear, while his fingers slide into my shorts and find my clit. I whimper as he starts talking and stroking.

"Your little pussy is so tight, I want to fuck it so hard. I love the feeling of my cock inside you. I want so badly to grip those beautiful curvy hips and drive into you until you can't breathe. I want you to wrap your lips around my cock and suck until I'm cumming so hard…"

I whimper and grip his shoulders, his finger moves faster and faster and I'm so close to the edge.

"Say my name, baby. Say it while you cum for me. Say it."

"Johnny," I gasp and shudder as an orgasm rips through my body.

"Fuckin' beautiful," he murmurs, kissing me again.

"How long until I can have you again?" I whisper, dropping my forehead to his.

"Right fuckin' now."

I pull back. "I'll hurt you…"

"Not if you ride me real slow."

The thought has my groin clenching again. I stand and slowly shimmy my shorts off. He watches me with a hungry expression as I remove my top and bra until I'm standing fully naked in front of him.

"Get over here," he growls.

I smile seductively and reach for his pants, gently lowering them and tossing them to the ground. He slides his hips forward and I straddle him, taking care not to lean on his stomach. I put my hands on his shoulders and slowly begin lowering myself onto his throbbing dick.

"Fuck," he hisses as I slowly slide down.

When I'm fully impaled, his eyes roll a little and his breathing quickens. I lift myself up and gently slide back down again, relishing in his cries of pleasure. I continue this pattern, gently rocking my hips until he's begging me for more. I love to hear him beg, it does crazy things to me.

"Tell me how good I feel?" I purr, in a husky voice.

"So fuckin' good. So fuckin' tight. God, you make me want to fuckin' cum so hard."

"Cum for me," I croon, rocking back and forth.

His jaw is tight, and his head is back, his hands are on my hips and his chest muscles are straining as he nears closer.

"Not until you," he rasps.

"This isn't for me."

"Fuck," he growls as he finally lets go.

His ragged groans fill my ears and bring me over the edge, I cum with him and we both cry out as my body milks him. When we come down from our high, I gently slide off him and pull on my clothes. He leans back, grinning lazily at me.

"Wipe that grin off your face, you animal," I laugh.

"I should get shot more often."

I give him a deadly look.

He yawns.

"Old man needs a nap after that?"

"Shut up," he murmurs.

"You should get some rest."

He nods and leans back down into the pillows, closing his eyes.

"I'll come by again later," I murmur, leaning down and kissing his mouth.

"Alright, night little girl," he rasps.

"It's not night, handsome."

He grins, keeping his eyes closed. I lean in and kiss him again, "Good day, Jagger."

~*~*~*~

The funeral is awful. My mother sobs loudly and clings to me, putting on a show that is fit for the best actors out there. I try hard to keep everything together. Jenny avoids her at all costs, the two of them having a relationship that is far beyond strained. When the coffin is lowered into the ground, I turn to my sister and hug her close.

It's over. It's really over.

Sarah tells my mother it's time to go and she turns to Jenny and I, her face scrunched as she takes us in. I know she's going to open her mouth and make even more of a scene, but I'm not going to take it. Not here. Not today.

"When will you two girls come and visit me more?"

Jenny looks away.

"We need time," I say, my voice careful. "Things aren't easy right now."

Her distraught green eyes meet Jenny's. "You forgave him, when will you forgive me?"

"Don't do this now," Jenny says gently. "I didn't forgive him. I didn't even get to speak to him. I'm not sure how I feel, but right now, I need space."

"You two are as selfish as ever," she snaps.

"Come on, let's get you back," Sarah says, taking my mom's hand.

"This isn't over," she tells us both as she is pulled back to the car. "You two girls are going to come and speak to me, and we're going to sort this out."

When she's gone, Jenny takes my hand, and we all make the journey back home. The funeral was small, basically just enough to do the right thing by him and ensure he got the burial he needed. When we return, Jagger is in the kitchen already making me a drink. He's all kinds of good. I don't know what I'd do without him.

"Are you ok?" he asks, handing it to me as he pulls me closer to him.

I nod. "I'm just glad it's over."

"I bet you are."

He leans down, kissing me in a way that makes me weak at the knees. A knock at the door sounds out just as he pulls away. I stare at Ava, and she shrugs, so I let go and walk over to see who it is. When I open it, I'm faced with a very beautiful woman. She's tall, with white blond hair and big brown eyes. She's quite possibly one of the most attractive women I've ever laid eyes on. She smiles at me, and I return it, wondering who she is?

"Holy shit," I hear Angel breathe from behind me. "What the fuck?"

"Angel, oh, it's you...I can't believe it."

Who is this woman?

Her eyes move past him and the expression on her face is enough to have me turning to see what she's looking at. Jagger is standing a few meters behind me holding a glass, and as though in slow motion, it slides from his hand and smashes on the floor. His eyes are red and glassy. Is Jagger *crying*? What the hell is going on? He chokes out some incoherent words and before I know it, the woman is shoving past me. She rushes towards him and throws herself into his arms.

I watch in utter horror and confusion as he wraps his arms around her and buries his face into her neck. My stomach turns and it feels like the world just slowly stops. Ava is standing beside me, I don't even know how she got there, her expression as confused as mine. When the two finally pull apart, Jagger looks her over. Maybe she's a good friend or something?

"You're alive. This is a fuckin' dream. What the hell is going on?"

Alive?

"I have been in protection. It's a long story, but I'm safe now. I'm safe. I'm home, baby. I'm home. The last three years of my life have been the hardest I've ever experienced, I never thought I'd get to see you again and now I can…"

"I thought you were dead," he says, his voice low and raspy. "I thought you were fuckin' dead. I mourned. I fuckin' died inside. All this time you've been right under my nose…"

"It was the only way. It was the only option. I was in danger. I'll explain it all later, I just," her voice breaks and she sobs, "I'm home."

This is bad. This is very very bad. Ava takes my hand and I use her to steady myself. Jagger looks past this woman and meets my gaze. There is so much written on his face, so many things he looks like he wants to say. I don't understand. Nothing about this is making any sense.

"Listen, you have to…" he begins, but she cuts him off.

"It doesn't matter. Nothing matters. I'm here. I'm home. God, my husband, my baby, I've missed you so much," she croaks, wrapping her arms around him again.

Husband?

Husband?

That's it for me, I reach down to the table by the door and take my keys. I need to get out of here. I can't hear any more of this. I can't even think. My mind is swimming as it tries to process what the hell just happened.

"Willow," Jagger yells.

I rush out the front door and onto the sidewalk, a moment later Jagger is behind me and gripping my arm, spinning me around to face him. His face is red, and his eyes are glassy, he's panting with a mixture of shock and rushing out to stop me.

"Wait. Let me explain. I didn't fuckin' know she was alive. I didn't...I thought she was dead."

"A wife?" I cry. "You have a wife and you never thought to mention that?"

"I thought she was dead," he answers, his face a whole lot paler than it was a few minutes ago, "I honestly thought she was dead. My mind is fuckin' swimming right now."

I have so many questions. So many things I want to say. I want to call him a liar because he never told me, never even thought to mention it. But I also feel incredibly selfish because it's hardly his fault. I can't think. The only thing that comes out is the question that doesn't really matter at this stage, and yet it's the only thing my brain will conjure up.

"Did you love her?"

"Yes."

"Do you still?"

He just stares at me. How is he supposed to answer that?

"My wife just came back from the dead," he whispers, "how can you ask me something like that?"

"You have a wife," I croak. "You're married, Jagger."

"Yeah."

"You didn't tell me that. You never thought to tell me that?"

"Jesus, I'm not going over this now. No, I didn't mention it. I don't fuckin' think it was relevant considering I thought she was fuckin' dead and it was one of the hardest times in my life."

My mind is spinning. I can't think.

I can barely breathe.

How can I be angry at him? I can't be. That wouldn't be fair. But I know I need to process this. I need to stop my mind from turning.

"What does this mean?" I ask, my voice shaky.

"I don't know. I don't know what it means."

Those words crush me, even though I don't blame him for them.

How can I?

I know what it feels like to see someone you thought was dead.

That someone is his wife.

Jagger has a wife.

Someone he loved.

Someone he wanted to share his life with.

And she's beautiful, so damned beautiful.

"I need to process this," he tells me, his voice defeated. "I'll take her home."

Home.

To his house.

To the house I spent so much time with him.

The place that brought us together and, funnily, the place that'll tear us apart.

I nod. It's all I can do.

"I'll go out so you can pack your things," I say, my voice hitching.

"Willow…"

I turn, without another word, and I walk away.

I just walk away.

There is nothing else to do.

Jagger has a wife.

A wife.

How am I supposed to live with that?

TO BE CONTINUED…